From *Playing With Fire: The Battle of the Bands*

Shivawn wandered, almost hypnotized, out to where she could see the man laying down that dark, thrumming, pelvis-churning bass.

After the rest of the band, she was expecting leather, tats, and metal makeup. But no, the bass player was a mysterious contradiction. He wore an ordinary black tee, but it stretched across his broad chest and bowling-ball-muscled shoulders like paint. His pants were regular jeans, not leather, and a bit white with wear, but molded to his legs like silk. His axe was nothing special, but something, the unusual tuning pegs or inlays or bridge pickup, told her this instrument was finer than it looked.

He was intent on his music, gaze on his bass as his long, artistic fingers glided easily along the fingerboard. Shivawn stood there, swaying, letting his music stir her. His notes reverberated deep inside her, where nothing else could touch. Her heart. Her soul. His hands were as capable on the guitar as they'd be on a woman's body. On *her* body.

Then he looked up.

Directly.

At.

Her.

His jet-black eyes burned with all the tightly leashed passion that he was pouring into his music.

Her breath left her. Her heart paused, on the brink of recognition.

His gaze focused entirely on her—and connected with her with an almost physical force.

Electricity surged through her, her whole body going haywire. Her heart beat a new, hummingbird's rhythm.

She swallowed hard. Ordinary? He was in no way ordinary.

But more...here was the band that could beat them.

RT Reviews TOP PICK "A must-read!" ~RT Reviews on *Passion Bites*

"[An] alpha male and sparky, feisty female with passion running hot..." ~Amazon 5-star review on *Hot Chips and Sand*

Playing With Fire: The Battle of the Bands

It's the Battle of the Bands, but the real battle is in their hearts.

An electric story of music, passion, family, and rivalry. USA Today Bestselling author Mary Hughes brings you an intimate glimpse into musicians' lives, with flashes of her signature humor.

Clumsy but smokin' fiddle-player Shivawn Kelly meets hot bass guitarist Connor Chase and lightning attraction strikes. But their bands are adversaries in the first Starstruck Battle of the bands. Only one can win.

Shivawn fervently hopes it's her family's céilí band, but Connor's rock group might just be better. His music stirs her soul even as his lithe body stirs her interest. But her da forbids her to even go near "that eejit boy".

Connor needs the win for his band to trust him again, but Shivawn and her music light his heart with joy. Yet when he tries to connect with her, she rebuffs him. He respects her need for distance, though it's tearing him up inside.

And then he overhears a rival band plotting—and he's afraid their target is Shivawn. He may have to defy her wishes, her father, and his even own band to keep her safe.

Welcome to STARSTRUCK, a showplace for talent, a playground for love. A collection of contemporary novellas that will leave you breathless and craving more.

Indulge and enjoy!

* * *

(novellas sold separately)

OBSESSED by Beth Ciotta
WRECKED by Cynthia Valero
JADED by Elle J Rossi
PLAYING WITH FIRE by Mary Hughes
CRUSHED by Elle J Rossi
DESIRED by Kathy Love

Look for these titles
by Mary Hughes

Now Available:

Romantic Adventure
Edie and the CEO—Crimson Romance
Falling ~~on~~ for the Billionaire
Cin Wikkid: April Fools For Love
Hot Chips and Sand
Bad Boy Billionaire's Lady: Lovless Brothers
Playing With Fire: The Battle of the Bands

Biting Love Series
Bite My Fire—Entangled
Biting Nixie—Entangled
The Bite of Silence—Entangled
Biting Me Softly—Entangled
Biting Oz—Entangled
Beauty Bites—Entangled
Downbeat—Entangled
Assassins Bite—Entangled
Passion Bites—Entangled
Biting Love Nibbles

Pull of the Moon Series

Prophecy Mates
Heart Mates
Hunt Mates
Mind Mates

The Ancients
Night's Caress

Standalone
Black Diamond Jinn

Coming Soon:

The Classic Billionaire's Newshound (Lovless Brothers)
The Genius Billionaire's Hacker (Lovless Brothers)
Night's Kiss (The Ancients)
Night's Bliss (The Ancients)
Soul Mates (Pull of the Moon)

Playing With Fire: The Battle of the Bands

A Starstruck Novella

Mary Hughes

DEDICATION

To Dan Lloyd, guitarist extraordinaire, who read my first book with a musician heroine, and when I asked how I'd done (secretly hoping for approval), he said something along the lines of, "I liked it!" then gently added, "But she didn't practice enough." Hoping Shivawn practices enough, lol.

To Brian K. for his insight on bass guitar.

To Stacy D. Holmes, who makes my stories shine. You give me a high bar to clear, but the hard work is always utterly worth it.

To EJR Digital Arts for the amazing cover. The story begins with your art.

To the Mary Hughes Readers groups, for your love and support.

Special thanks to the fabulous Stasi Swain for vetting the ending.

To the 2018 Starstruck crew, Elle J Rossi and Kathy Love. Thanks to Elle J Rossi for inviting me to be part of this brilliant universe!

As always, to Gregg. For being with me, even those blurry mornings when Jingle Bells in whole notes is a bit of an artistic stretch and my funniest joke is, "Knock, knock." "Who's there?" "Me."

Chapter One

Line dancing was harder than it looked. Shivawn Kelly had heard musicians were supposed to be more coordinated than most. Not her. Apparently, while the Fiddle Fairy had been fussing over her, the Klutz Fairy had taken a free shot.

"Why are we dancing, again?" she asked as she stumbled into Cousin Margaret a fourth time. "We're supposed to be scoping out the competition."

"We *are* inspecting the competition. Very thoroughly."

Her cousin's gaze ran over the lead singer onstage, going all dreamy at his skinny jeans and cowboy hat. Her eyes, the aching blue of a summer sky filled with mare's-tail clouds, did the dreamy look really well. Maggie had a true Irish lass's coloring with her translucent skin and rose-gold hair. Shivawn was her mirror image, if the mirror was old and darkened—chestnut-red hair, green eyes, and skin that sort of tanned before it burned.

"Maggie, dear, it's amazing how much scoping out the competition looks like ogling the singer."

"Oh, pooh. I don't always go for the lead singer."

She cut a disbelieving glance at her cousin, which sent her off-kilter and knocking into Maggie again. *But really, this time she deserved it.* "Margaret Clancy. You always told me there are only three kinds of band groupies: the ones swooning at the singer's crooning; the ones dazzled by the lead guitar's brilliant riffs; and the ones who want to do the drummer for his obvious hand-eye coordination."

"So, which are you?" she shot back.

Shivawn kept her eyes glued to her feet. "None of the above. I'm surprised you're interested. Musicians know how shallow the glamour is. Even a flute player is a musician, of sorts."

"Ha, ha."

But if I had to pick, give me the bass guitar every time. Not obvious or showy, the bass guitar was steady and relentless and drove the whole group to its climax. *Give me that in bed any day over showy or self-absorbed.*

Shivawn glanced at the electric bass in this country band. The grizzled blond competently walked fingers up and down the fretboard. Decent enough. But even if her eyes were capable of dreamy, which they weren't, she wouldn't have gone gooey over him.

The glimpse distracted her long enough that she grapevined left as Cousin Margaret went right, and she ran into her for the umpteenth time.

Fed up, Shivawn grabbed Maggie's elbow and pulled her out of line—apparently a mortal sin from the black glares she got. But, really. Just because she didn't have her cousin's fairy skin didn't mean she didn't bruise.

She hauled them off the dance floor to the nearest bar. Bar—the word usually brought images of a narrow, gloomy space, a band smashed in a tiny corner, a postage-size dance floor, and cramped seating. But this was Starstruck, a combo dance club/concert hall, and everything was huge. Big stage, gigantic dance floor, sweeping balcony, and not one but two bars.

As Shivawn crossed the dance floor to what could've been the next county, she managed to finish her thought. "What do you think of the band?"

"As a musician *of a sort*," Maggie began, proving she *had* been listening instead of ogling, or at least listening in addition to ogling, "it's my opinion that, despite Hotty McCowboy's many attractions, our band is better." Her lilting Celtic accent made it sound less like bragging and more like a kindness.

Shivawn had no such lilt. Though her da was Irish, and she'd been born there, her mother was all American. At five, because of her parents' separating, she'd been whisked to the USA to grow up here with her mother. Now her accent was firmly Midwest.

So, when she said, "Yeah," it was flatter than a pancake. "So far I haven't seen or heard anyone who comes close to giving our kind of show."

Which was important, because Shivawn and her family band were here to compete in the first annual Starstruck Battle of the Bands.

At the east bar, a truly spectacular bartender was handing out drinks and a sizzling smile with equal speed and flair. The man packaged sex appeal like a Ferrari. Within moments, he slid toward them. He wore the Starstruck uniform of a black T-shirt with logo. But on him, it looked like less of a uniform and more of a tribute.

"What can I get you ladies?" The rich timbre of his voice, the lyrical spin he put on his words, caressed her ears. She bet he was a singer.

"I'll have your best beer on tap," Shivawn said, then pointed to her cousin. "She'll have some sissy drink."

"They're not sissy," Maggie objected. "They have *flavor*." She turned her brightest smile on Mr. Tall, Dark, and Drinksome. "I'll sample whatever you're mixing up tonight." A bump of her strawberry brows gave "mixing" a bit of added steam.

"Well. For you..." Hands spread on the bar, he leaned toward them, chest and arm muscles bulging appealingly as he added his own bit of steam. "We're having a special on margaritas."

"Sold." Maggie mirrored his tilt, plumping her considerable assets in her V-neck sweater. "Margarita is like my name, you know. Margaret, margarita."

"Mine's Ben." As he tapped his name badge hanging from a blue lanyard, his gaze stayed on Maggie's.

Shivawn gave him points for that. Her cousin had a flutist's truly spectacular chest.

"Done with singers?" she murmured, and Maggie shot her an I-will-shortsheet-your-bed look. Shivawn smiled innocently.

"As far as beer goes," Ben spoke to her this time while his hands nimbly prepared the margarita. "All our beers are the best."

"What's your favorite, then? I'll have that."

"One dopplebock coming up." He smoothly slid a jumbo margarita before Cousin Margaret then retrieved a glass and frosted beer bottle, uncapped, and expertly poured.

As Ben moved off to serve other customers, Shivawn cast her gaze around the large space. On the main stage, the country band twanged its last number. Another band was setting up on the smaller, temporary stage across the dance floor from the first, tucked in beside the bar where Shivawn sampled a truly lovely dark beer. The two stages were alternating hopefuls of all genres in the four days of open auditions. Her family's band was scheduled for the final night of preliminaries. Three judges, currently anonymous, would pick the top bands to go on. Things would get cooking with the first bracket playoffs Thursday.

"Where do you think the judges are?"

"Maybe in the balcony?" Margaret turned away from the bar and leaned back on her elbows, surveying the exposed second floor to her right. Her gaze wandered to the temporary stage, where the new band, lots of leather, skin, and studs, finished setting up. As the country band struck its final chord, she went on, "Or maybe the judges are dancing—"

"Weren't they good?" A blond guy on the second stage grabbed a mic and broke into the dying chord. "Put your hands together for Country Boys and Cowboy Boots." He raised his arms over his head and mimicked clapping.

Shivawn knew it was mimicked because if he'd really clapped, the amplified thud-thud-thud would've burned out their eardrums.

Applause like a brief rain spattered an instant before the guy said, "Now get ready to rock your body down with Taboo Soul."

He flipped his long blond hair back, and Shivawn would have sworn she heard three women around her sigh.

Onstage, the lead guitar dashed off a riff that could've made Jimi Hendrix cry, a virtuoso run of tangling fingers, accompanied by muscular poses worthy of a superhero. He ended on a dramatic, dominant seventh chord that poised them all at the top of the song's cliff.

And then the bass guitar came in with a glide from *sol* to *do,* so smooth and perfect it ran along Shivawn's flesh like silk, leaving her skin rumpled and aching. When the drummer hit the first beat, everyone was hooked.

But for her, she'd been hooked by that bass slide.

The singer started rasping out lyrics as the crowd cheered. Shivawn's feet carried her away from the bar, out to where she could see past the blond throwing his long hair around as he deep-throated the mic. Past the shaved-skull lead guitarist jumping around the stage like a stringy Hulk. Past the biker-styled rhythm guitar stalking in his wake. She wandered, almost hypnotized, out to where she could see the man laying down that dark, thrumming, pelvis-churning bass.

After the rest of the band, she was expecting leather, tats, and metal makeup. But no, the bass player was a mysterious contradiction. He wore an ordinary black tee, but it stretched across his broad chest and bowling-ball-muscled shoulders like paint. His pants were regular jeans, not leather, and a bit white with wear, but molded to his legs like silk. His axe was nothing special—black body, maple fretboard, silver bridge and controls. But something, the unusual tuning pegs or inlays or bridge pickup, told her this instrument was finer than it looked.

Cousin Margaret's voice, calling her name, fell muffled on her ears as her feet brought her closer yet. She'd expected leather, and certainly those powerful arms and strong legs would look great encased in lots of buttery black...or better yet, nothing at all.

He was intent on his music, gaze on his bass as his long, artistic fingers glided easily along the fingerboard. While the lead singer vacationed on an ego trip, and the lead guitar put so many riffs in inappropriate places he began to sound like aural tinsel, the bassist hung out in the back— controlling the pace and shape of the music. Steady. Sure. Never changing.

No, scratch that. He was, ever so slightly, pushing the beat, slowly increasing both tempo and volume, but almost unnoticeably. The audience would feel it as a rising temperature in the room, a quickening of heartbeats. Without fanfare, but as sure as the dawn, he brought both music and audience slowly and inevitably to their feet.

Shivawn stood there, swaying, letting his music stir her. She didn't understand her reaction, as he seemed mostly ordinary. Yet his notes reverberated deep inside her, where nothing else could touch. Her heart. Her soul. His hands were as capable on the guitar as they'd be on a woman's body. On *her* body.

Then he looked up.

Directly.

At.

Her.

His jet-black eyes burned with all the tightly leashed passion that he was pouring into his music.

Her breath left her. Her heart paused, on the brink of recognition.

His gaze focused entirely on her—and connected with her with an almost physical force.

Electricity surged through her, her whole body going haywire. Her heart beat a new, hummingbird's rhythm.

She swallowed hard. Ordinary? He was in no way ordinary.

But more...here was the band that could beat them.

Chapter Two

"*Siobhán,*" an angry Irish tenor burred behind her. "*What* the feck do you think you're doing, staring at those boys like an eejit?"

At first Shivawn didn't know the voice was talking to her. Then she didn't understand why.

The *who* cut through, though.

She spun, suppressing a dozen conflicted feelings. "Da." Despite being "Shivawn" on everything from birth certificate to Social Security card, her father insisted on pronouncing and spelling her name the traditional way.

"You're staring up there at that sodding band like the cat stares at cream. They're our feckin' enemies, Siobhán."

Their competition, yes. But enemies? When they could make music like this? When just the pump and slide of fingers on fretboard of one of them could trigger the pump and slide of her heart?

"It's...he's..." She tried to explain, but when she needed her tongue the most, it ended up being even clumsier than her feet. "It's not what it looks like, Da."

"It's exactly what it looks like! Come away from there."

He grabbed her arm as the song hit the refrain and rainbows burst from a nearby light panel. She turned to keep watching the band. Red, blue, and green flashes stop-motioned the musicians, peak snapshots of intense faces and flying fingers, visually highlighting their force and drive as their music did aurally.

Walking backwards, she gaped as the band's lighting guy did a fabulous, innovative light show. "Da, wait. We could learn something from them."

He stopped and shook her arm to turn her toward him. "Now listen here. The only thing you learn from your enemy is how to defeat them."

She couldn't let that ride a second time. "They're not our enemies. They're good musicians, and that guitarist has amazing musical ideas, fresh and alive, techniques that I could apply to being a better fiddle—"

"You stay away from that eejit boy." Da's hand shot out, waving at the lead guitar, though she'd meant the bass. "He'll fill your head with nonsensical noodles, not nice clean cuts and rolls." Céilí band cuts and rolls, he meant. Music the way heaven intended.

The lead guitarist was at that moment cascading out notes with such frantic abandon they made no musical sense, so in one way she had to agree with her father. But they were energetic enough to get the even unmusical in the crowd cheering, something Da could learn from.

"Not everything new is wrong, Da—"

"Feck, Siobhán. These boys are giving you strange notions, more than usual. We're named the Kelly Traditional Céilí Band for a reason—we have a certain sound, and it's based on tradition. You stray from tradition, you change our sound."

Is that such a bad thing? She opened her mouth to ask it but already knew the answer. The Kelly band began with

Da's mam and da. Questioning the value of tradition was like questioning the value of family.

A sore point, since her mother had split open their family with a rift that was an ocean wide. Though Shivawn hadn't had a choice in leaving him, she was happy growing up—and had always felt a vague guilt about that. To make up for it, she tried to do what he said, to make him happy. So she answered the only way she could. "Yes, Da."

"Then you'll stay away from that eejit boy?"

"I'll stay away." She sighed. She'd stay away from the bassist, even though they'd both be here for hours each day, listening to the competition. Even though they were all staying in the same hotel just a mile away.

But I can avoid one man, right?

A momentary gap in the dancing crowd revealed the dark, powerful bass guitarist.

His gaze met hers—and she read there that if he had his way, avoiding him wasn't going to be as easy as she thought.

*   *   *

Connor Chase stood easily on the stage behind the showier members of Taboo Soul and crafted a bass line to drive the music to its conclusion. He kept his gaze locked on the pretty redhead getting towed by what looked like a leprechaun's version of a drill sergeant.

He'd been totally focused on the music, matching drummer Zach's steady pace while adding enough forward movement to keep the music flowing, when he'd looked up, straight into the brightest green eyes he'd ever seen.

Lovely, lovely eyes, but more.

The woman possessing them hadn't been watching their frontman Daw flip his salon-perfect hair or even the lead guitarist with his finger pyrotechnics.

She'd been staring right at Connor.

That juiced him. But even better, she didn't ogle him as if he were a sex machine strapped into a guitar. No, her gaze had been on his face, her body swaying with, not the beat but the phrases. As if she saw the music in his head, as if she understood exactly what he was doing.

Lightning streaked through him. *She gets me.*

Then he snorted to himself. *As if.* Six months ago, he found out how easy it was to lose trust and understanding—even from a supposed friend. These days, he was playing with the group on sufferance. He needed to drive them to a win, to get their trust back.

Still, the heat from the redhead's gaze, that insane electric connection, fired Connor up, so that he pushed the music harder and higher than he'd ever done before. As they struck the final chord, the audience went wild. Even Zach gave him a wow-well-done raised eyebrow and nod.

And Connor knew he had to meet that woman.

The instant they were done, he jumped off the stage, rushing to look for her before he even put away his guitar and amp.

But she was gone.

*　　*　　*

Shivawn began the next day with the best of eejit-boy-avoiding intentions. Her plan was simple: hide out in her hotel room until it was time for the Kelly band to take the stage.

She breakfasted on cereal bars in the room she shared with Cousin Margaret. The Kramer Hotel was midtown, with Starstruck on the outskirts of the little Illinois burg. All the bands were staying in a block of rooms here, with three charter buses driving between the hotel and the bar several times a day.

Shivawn practiced with her mute on until lunch, then ate at a nearby diner with her da. A few young men from other bands wandered near, as if they'd possibly strike up a conversation, only to be stopped dead by her father's glare.

Thank you, Da. She sighed. Some fathers met potential suitors for their daughters with a shotgun in their lap. Da's eyes fired buckshot.

She managed to get through the whole day without one glimpse of the Taboo Soul bassist.

Ah, hell. Maybe I'm making too big a deal of it. As she boarded the bus with her fiddle, she shook her head. *He probably doesn't even remember me.*

At Starstruck, she and the rest of the family left their cases in a guarded room off a back hallway, probably normally used for storage, set up for all the bands. Then, with an hour until their turn, she and Maggie went to the main room to spend the time sizing up the last of their competition.

Shivawn was at the edge of the dance floor, moving with the beat of a steel drum band but not actually dancing, when her nape tightened, the small hairs rising as if in the presence of a coming storm. She turned.

There he was.

Last night, the bass player had worn a thin tee and jeans, the better to show off his body moving with the music. Tonight, he was wearing exactly what she'd first imagined him in.

He was even more impressive in street clothes.

A black leather jacket emphasized the breadth of his shoulders. Its open front showcased his spectacular chest and abs in a tight burgundy T-shirt. Black jeans encased his hips. He looked very dangerous and desirable indeed.

Her whole body trembled, seeing him standing there, lean and rangy and at his lethal ease.

When his head turned, their gazes met across the room, and her blood lit with fire.

Then he started toward her. Coming *for* her.

Her heart pounded fast, nearly out of her chest.

Remember your promise to Da, she coached herself. *Get out of here.*

But she couldn't help lingering a moment longer, her gaze feasting on the man stalking across the room like a panther. She imagined what she might say to him if he actually reached her. Words of admiration, coy flirting... Yet knowing, in reality, her stumbling tongue would spoil everything.

That, finally, cut through the excited muddle that was her brain.

Shivawn spun and fled to hide in the ladies' restroom.

Half an hour later, Cousin Margaret slapped open the door. "*There* you are. Two minutes. Hurry!"

Shivawn crept out to see her family had set up on the main stage. She dashed for the storage room, bumped her way through several people trying to jitterbug, and managed to finally get to where she'd stowed her fiddle case. Throwing it open, she snatched up instrument and bow, checked the tuning on the run with a quick plink of strings, and slipped through the crowd again to the stage. Somehow, with the fiddle in her hands, she never had to worry about stuttering feet and easily leaped onto the platform to take her place.

"About time," Da muttered.

With a deep breath to slow her heart and calm herself, she clamped the fiddle under her jaw to free her hands to tension the bow hair. No clip mic for her instrument, because Da didn't believe in artificial amplification. Only the three standing mics at the edge of the darkened stage, courtesy of the management no doubt. She stood, bow in hand, listening to the final notes of a pretty good forties-style big band. Somewhere out there were three judges, evaluating them. About to evaluate her.

And *him*. He was out there, too, the dangerous bass. But she wasn't thinking about him. *Much.*

Once the big band finished, Cousin Liam flipped the automatic light switch as Da took center stage. "The Kelly Traditional Céilí Band," he boomed, spinning his syllables with an over-the-top Irish brogue.

He lives for this.

Hundreds of expectant faces turned toward them—three of which could make or break her family's chances to advance to the next round. Only twenty bands would be chosen from the hundreds of hopefuls.

But suddenly, Shivawn didn't care. She was about to make music.

She loved the press of strings denting her fingertips as the notes flowed from under her hand. Loved the vibration and resonance of the fiddle, filling with sound until it overflowed, singing out into the crowd. Standing limber and ready, she couldn't wait to start.

Da tapped out the beat on his bodhrán. As he *dum*-da-dum-i-ta'd through an opening bar, Aunt Katie filled her accordion with air, Cousin Margaret drew breath, Uncle

Seamus lifted his spoon-shaped dulcimer mallets, and Liam pressed fingers to his mandolin's fretboard. Shivawn raised her bow.

Beat one came again, and they were off.

The opening song was her favorite, "Cooley's Reel." Up-tempo, alternating eighths and triplets, plenty of good places for what Cousin Liam, who was studying at the conservatory, called melismata, and she called fancy fingering. Spirited and lively, the reel was a surefire kickstart to the audience's blood.

Sure enough, within a few bars, heads were nodding, feet were tapping, and some of the more adventurous were trying to fit dance steps to the tune.

A good sign. While only the three unknown judges decided who entered the bracket elimination, if the Kelly band made it to the final round, they'd also be judged based on audience popularity.

Having three songs to win the judges' hearts, they followed the reel with what Liam called "Irish Tune from County Derry," Da called "Derry Air," and those of them raised in the Midwest US called "Danny Boy."

Da crooned a mean tear-jerker, and there wasn't a dry eye in the house by the ballad's end. Her chest swelled with pride.

"Leave 'em dancing and wanting more", that was Da's motto, and Granda's before him. *"'Tis the Kelly way,"* Da often said, and experience proved he was right.

They finished with a medley of jigs, each faster than the last. By the end, the whole bar was whirling out of control. Shivawn pranced and spun as if leading them. In a line with other people, she couldn't dance worth a dung beetle, but up here, she could jig, reel, and waltz with the best of them.

She finished the last note with a flourish of bow, the grand gesture a reflection of her delight with a grand performance. Not worried at all now because the clapping and cheering had already begun.

The applause was lovely, fast and loud, the rising pitch a show of true enthusiasm. Performance, for her, was about connecting with listeners, and tonight's appreciation rang like a peal of bells in her ears, echoing the joy in her heart.

Sweaty but satisfied, Shivawn hopped down from the stage.

Nearly crashing into a hard, dark, male body. Strong hands clamped around her upper arms, steadying her. Shockwaves of heat and pleasure rocked her at the clasp.

She lifted her eyes as the hands released her. A dark, intelligent gaze met hers.

It was the bassist from Taboo Soul.

Chapter Three

Shivawn's whole body went on red alert.

Inches from her, his height was intimidating. His muscles begged for her touch. His eyes were a brilliant near-black—and focused totally on *her*. She sucked in a shocked breath and experienced one thing more—his heady masculine scent.

"Wh-what...?" she stuttered. *What do you want with me? What did you think of us? What will you do to me?* All those and more, but her voice wouldn't work past the first word. Apparently, the fiddle only worked its magic on her feet.

"My name's Connor. Connor Chase."

His voice was a gorgeous bass as rich as his instrument, and it stirred her flesh like the caress of cashmere.

"I saw you yesterday during our set. I tried to talk with you then."

She shook her head, her gaze helplessly ensnared by his. She meant, *No, we can't talk, we're rival groups, enemies even*, but he must've taken it as, *No, I didn't see you,* because he went on.

"I felt like you were really listening. Really getting my music."

Her gut lurched, but there was more.

"Hearing you play, well." He touched her hand. "Now I know why the feeling was so strong."

Though his warm fingertips were feather-light on her skin, she knew the strength in his hand—from ten thousand hours plus of practice—would be great, and somehow, she could feel every bit of his power. Closing her eyes, she flew to heaven for a brief time on the wings of his sure touch.

Behind her, Da cleared his throat. She knew it was him because he could even *ahem* in Irish.

"Come away from here, Siobhán. There's practicing to be done before tomorrow."

Her heart fell, and she opened her eyes with a gut-wrenching sigh. To the bassist, she said in a low voice, "I'm sorry. You've imagined any connection between us. We're competitors. Don't come after me again," then spun on her heel to prove it to both of them, breaking the physical connection of his hand.

She lurched into the crowd, thinning now as the dancers amoebaed toward the second stage. Da followed. But something drew her back to *him*, to Connor, and she glanced over her shoulder—and stumbled. Embarrassed, she snapped forward and barged her way through to the cooler air of the hallway leading to storage.

Where she dared another glance back.

Connor stood amid the moving crowd, not swayed in the least, a frown darkening his features as he stared after her.

Heat kindled deep inside; her heart beat faster, and she took a single step toward him.

"Come along, Siobhán." Her da's tone was sharp as he breezed past her.

Only three days to go. Turning away from Connor and temptation, she fixed her gaze on Da's plaid vest and followed him into the back.

Surely she could be strong for just three more days.

*   *   *

Thursday morning, Shivawn woke excited and scared. Today, Starstruck's owner would post which bands were going on to the next round.

Today they'd find out if they'd made the cut.

She set the small pot of coffee on to perk then jumped in the shower as Cousin Margaret yawned awake. Normally Shivawn wouldn't have worried. The Kelly band toured every summer and had won countless competitions at the national level. Hell, they'd played a coveted gig at Milwaukee's Irishfest. They were the best of the best.

This was different.

She squeezed a dollop of golden shampoo from the hotel's small bottle to wash her hair. Sure, Kramer was a dot on the map—one of the smallest US towns west of the Pacific. Its county, Grundy, wasn't much bigger, at a shade over fifty thousand people, tiny compared to next-door-neighbor Cook's five million. A person might think the First Annual Battle of the Bands would be small potatoes.

Except for Rusty Ann Baker.

The country music legend was now in her early fifties, but somehow, since she gave up packing stadiums for owning a music bar, she'd become even more charismatic. Starstruck regularly featured big-name headliners. The

Battle had drawn bands from all across North America and as far away as Brazil, the UK, and Japan.

Working up a lather of soap on a pristine white washcloth, Shivawn scrubbed. The prizes were also commensurate with Rusty's reputation. Fifth through tenth place got showcase gigs at various Chicago venues, including the United Center, The Metro, and Schubas. Fourth place was a showcase at Starstruck itself. Third place got the same plus a month-long tour, all expenses paid. Second place got everything plus opening for Rusty if she did a farewell tour.

First place got all of that...plus a *recording contract*.

She leaped out of the shower, briskly toweled off, and threw on clothes while Maggie showered. Shivawn poured herself a cup of coffee but was too excited to eat, even a breakfast bar. Da salivated for that recording contract like Pavlov's dogs gone Niagara Falls. Sure, he might have been able to scrape together recording time from the money they spent flying back and forth over the Atlantic— Shivawn was based in the US—but they got most of their airfare on frequent flyer miles courtesy of Uncle Seamus's business, so maybe not. But even if they'd had the cash, Rusty's recording contract was with a capital-L Label, adding cachet and the all-important world-wide distribution.

So, bright and early that Thursday morning, every single band loaded onto the buses, even though second-round eliminations wouldn't play until tonight—and many wouldn't play at all.

Shivawn's bus pulled up a few minutes later in front of Starstruck's huge building. The normally blinding pink neon sign was dark, but her gaze and the gazes of everyone else on the bus immediately glued to the pages papering the front wall, a dozen copies of the same twenty-slot bracket. She could see the chart outline from here, but not the band names.

Heart pounding, she piled off with the rest and joined the crowd scanning the lists.

Twenty bands. *Are we one of them?* She edged closer.

When she finally spotted their name, she trilled, "There!"

Cousin Liam and Uncle Seamus saw it, too, and whooped. "We made it!" The rest of the family was as excited as she.

Well, most of them.

"Why are we third?" Da thumped one of the pages. "We were best. Why aren't we seeded first? And just who the flowery bollocks is The Beachies?"

"Who knows?" Cousin Margaret yawned. She'd hooked up with the lead singer from Country Boys and Cowboy Boots, whom she'd nicknamed Footlong—which Shivawn assumed was his shoe size or she'd have had to bleach her mind. Da hadn't chastised Maggie, but then again, the Country Boys probably hadn't made the cut so weren't their "feckin' enemies."

Speaking of...heart hammering in her throat, Shivawn checked the other groups on the list. The Kelly band playoff was against Windy City's Eagle's Wings, either a Gospel group or a much better name for a country band.

She skipped down the list, landing almost immediately on Taboo Soul—number nine, bracketed against ten's Levan Polkka.

Only after she'd found it did she even acknowledge to herself that she'd been looking for it.

"Stay away from that eejit boy." Easier promised than done, especially with her subconscious rooting for said eejit.

And just at that moment, when her subconscious was fixated on a forbidden boy, who should break loose of the mob around the lists but the leather-clad members of Taboo Soul.

The band plus a techie-looking guy in glasses, probably their lighting guy, came sauntering toward her. Her stomach swooped, recognizing Connor's black head above the rest, broad shoulders slightly rolled because his hands were in his jeans pockets and his head was down against the wind. So he hadn't seen her yet.

Stop staring. There's still time to look away…

She couldn't. As he walked toward her, her heart beat faster. *Closer, closer…*

And then his gaze flicked to her, hung a moment on hers, his step hesitating.

Her whole being clung to an invisible wire singing between them.

With a glint of anguish, he tore his gaze away. Sliding past her, his hands jammed even deeper in his pockets. From the wretchedness on his face, he wasn't hunched with early morning chill but against the pain of having to walk on by. He and his whole band passed her, headed for the nearby twenty-four-hour diner.

Her heart echoed his pain even as a gratitude swept her. Despite obviously wishing differently, he'd respected her request to stay away. Why couldn't she simply be glad at that?

"She's coming out," someone yelled.

Shivawn stuffed the conflicted feelings way down inside and looked back in time to see one of Starstruck's doors open. Rusty herself emerged.

The redhead was a small woman with a big presence. People crowding the doors and walls almost automatically moved a step or two back, as if shifted by her invisible bubble of charisma.

Smiling graciously, she moved among the bands, congratulating some, commiserating with others, until she reached Shivawn's family.

"Paddy Kelly, you old son of a bitch. I've been dying to meet you." She grabbed his hand and pumped it while Da appeared uncharacteristically shocked silent. "Nice singing last night. I especially liked how you didn't blast the climax of 'Danny Boy.' The most overdone song in the history of overdone songs. So many folks just scrabble up for that sixth like they're storming a castle and bust that high note like a smashed punkin'. But you, you made it aching, beautiful. Have breakfast with me?"

"Y-yes, ma'am. I-I'd be honored." What could he say after a tribute like that?

Well, shake my tambourine. Maybe I come by my stumble-bumbling naturally. Shivawn, having only seen her da as the infallible band leader, was tickled at this sign of a softer side.

Rusty linked arms with him and tugged him toward the diner.

Shivawn's appetite had returned, and she eagerly followed, heart beating harder. *Connor is in there.* She virtuously told herself she wouldn't seek him out.

But the moment she entered, the rest of the Kelly band behind her, Rusty waved at Connor's group sitting at a middle table. "Taboo Soul. Meet the Kelly Traditional Céilí

Band. One of the reasons I sponsored this shindig was to help musicians from different genres get acquainted. So folks, let's get acquainted." She flicked a commanding forefinger at the tables. "Push some of these together. Let's make a party."

As Connor and the guy Shivawn recognized as their drummer rose and pushed together a couple more tables, she was sure Da would've backed out or made some excuse. But Rusty was a force of nature, blowing them toward Connor's group. Then somehow, everyone was sitting but for Shivawn and Rusty.

And the two open chairs were beside Da—and Connor.

Dutifully, Shivawn went to sit beside her da, but Rusty elbowed her aside and scooted past, claiming it first. "Paddy Kelly, I've heard you're the man to tell me all about céilí bands." She slid into the chair beside him, throwing a quick twinkle over her shoulder at Shivawn.

Who just stood there, dumbfounded, not quite knowing what to do.

Da leaned out from behind Rusty and scowled, but the singer snared his attention with her country charm. "Darlin', tell me more about the drum you play. What's that called again? Bodice, bodycam…?"

She was laying it on a little thick but Da simply *tsked* and said, "Bodhrán."

Rusty nodded, then shot another glance over her shoulder at her and cut a nod at the empty chair beside Connor.

Left with one empty chair, Shivawn had little choice.

She perched next to him with a nervous little smile and a whole flood of stomach acid. Her heart pounded far out of proportion with the simple breakfast meet.

Breathe, Shivawn, breathe.

Mistake. He smelled even better than yesterday, all fresh from the shower. For a moment, the mental image of him stepping from the shower snared her. *Droplets of water trickling down the curve of his chest. Her, tracing the path with her tongue...*

Da leaned out and scowled.

Heat rose up her neck and face, and she cleared her throat as she pulled in her chair. "So wh-what's good here?" Her mouth didn't work right, but she covered with a bright smile at everyone and anyone who wasn't currently starring in her mental porn flick, aka Connor the Lickable.

One of the consequences of stumbling over your tongue was other people were usually too embarrassed or pitying to take you seriously. Nobody paid her any attention.

Nobody except Connor. He shot her a brief, almost unnoticeable commiserating glance before turning from her to start a conversation with Cousin Liam on his other side. "Nice energy in your band."

Irony. When the only person who *can't* notice you is the only one who does.

Uncle Seamus, on her other side, handed her a menu. "You can't go wrong with scrambled eggs and hash browns." He pronounced it "scurr-ambled" and "burr-owans," really trying to nail the American "R." He was a Clancy, and as Irish as her da, but he loved American television and his hero was Hugh Laurie. Every time he was on this side of the ocean, he tried out his American accent. "If Hugh can do it, I can." It made her smile.

Carafes of coffee arrived, dark, hot, and strong. Like Connor...

Though she kept up a conversation with her uncle, her mind was on the bassist beside her, and half an ear, too as Liam asked Connor what he played.

"Electric bass. You play mandolin."

He'd noticed?

True, musicians tended to associate the player with the instrument played, but they also tended to be absorbed in making their own music. Connor had demonstrated a level of observance above average.

"I do," her cousin replied. "I'm actually studying at the Royal College of Music." Ever diffident, Liam made this sound like Joe's Bar & Grill & Music Academy.

But Connor reacted with a, "Wow. That's a heavy hitter. Congratulations."

It *was* a heavy hitter, one of the best in the UK. Shivawn was impressed that Connor knew that. The fact that his admiration wasn't hampered by any wet blanket of ego impressed her even more.

They ordered, and plates came quickly. As the meal progressed, so did the conversation beside her.

"So, now, the mandolin," Connor said in his resonant bass, the timbre thrumming pleasantly through her. "It's tuned like a violin, right?"

"Right. How did you know that?"

"Oh, I'm interested in all stringed instruments."

Like mine? Her belly quivered.

Then he added, "For example, violins—you call them fiddles, right? Fiddle and electric bass strings are tuned exactly opposite—as if they're the perfect complement."

Fiddle and bass, a perfect complement? Her head jerked involuntarily around.

His gaze flicked toward her, so fast she almost thought she'd imagined it, but for a tiny smile on his lips.

"Electric guitar," Liam said. "A solid slab of wood, right? How do you deal with an instrument that doesn't resonate?"

Good question. Bowing a fiddle set the whole thing vibrating. She heard an up-close version of what the audience got. Plucking an electric bass without the amplifier made a sound like a fat rubber band.

"You learn to feel the music's vibration through the strings," he explained. "I use big, thick strings with a lot of slap just for that purpose. But speaking of electric…your mandolin sounds nice up close, but it's no match for the modern flute and fiddle. Why don't you amplify it?"

Also a good question, and one Shivawn had asked Da many times. They all knew the answer by now, and Liam gave it. "Amplification isn't traditional. I compensate with louder strings." He leaned closer to Connor, and she had to perk her ears to hear him add, "Though sometimes in private, I tune like a guitar and pretend I'm a rock star."

"Huh," Connor responded.

For a moment she was disappointed that he was brushing off Liam's dreams. Then he went on.

"I have my own deep, dark secret. In high school, I learned enough lute to play for the Madrigal dinner."

They both laughed at that, and a happy little trill vibrated deep inside Shivawn.

Da had scheduled a rehearsal at ten, so she didn't linger over breakfast. Connor's band apparently had the same idea, and everyone rose from the table at the same time.

They'd asked for two separate checks, but Rusty snatched both. "I'll take care of this."

Shivawn thanked her, grateful. Contrary to Hollywood depictions, musicians didn't get paid well—and most of what they did get went into instruments.

As she headed out with the rest, another group came in. Rusty waved at them. "Everyone, this is The Battre. They're a Beatles tribute band."

Connor took a single step in Shivawn's direction, drawing her attention. He was frowning.

She followed his gaze to a small man in a skinny suit and tie, his camel-brown hair in a long bowl haircut. He stared with visible malice at them.

No. Stared at—her.

Chapter Four

Connor left the diner with mixed feelings. While he'd enjoyed his conversation with Liam Clancy to a surprising degree, it had pained him to sit beside Shivawn and not be able to talk to her. To connect with her. To touch her.

He respected her wish not to get involved with a rival band member. So he'd stood aside, though it was hard.

But this morning, well, he hadn't missed her father's black glare at anyone and everyone who dared look upon his daughter with even a healthy interest. He began to wonder how much of Shivawn's hesitance actually came from Paddy Kelly.

Connor leaned against the diner's wall while the Kelly band boarded the first bus. As he'd finished breakfast, he'd considered maybe approaching her after the competition was over, to see if she might really be interested—and then he'd seen that Battre guitar player's dark, almost threatening stare.

Sure, maybe the man had simply been sizing up the competition. But Connor hadn't liked the calculating, malicious gleam when he'd targeted Shivawn.

Connor had taken an automatic, protective step toward her. Opened his mouth to warn her.

And would she believe you? Or would she hate you for interfering, like Daw?

His fists clenched in his jacket pockets. He *still* wanted to warn her, but experience had taught him a harsh lesson.

He and Daw and Zach had been best friends since grade school. Not so long ago, Connor had discovered Daw's girlfriend was trying to trap him into marriage. He told the Taboo Soul's lead singer that. He thought he was doing his friend a favor.

He'd been a naïve idiot.

He'd been sitting low on a couch in the garage where they rehearsed, thinking he was alone, listening to the music in his head, trying to find a better bass line. The rest of the band had been out on a beer run.

Daw's woman, talking on her phone just outside the garage, hadn't seen him. And by the time he came out of his head, she'd already said too much.

Shivawn's bus, with a belch of smoke, took off for the hotel. Another bus arrived in its wake. Connor boarded, his head still wrapped in the misery of memory.

"I went off the pill," Daw's woman said into her phone. "What Daw doesn't know won't hurt him."

He threw himself into an empty seat and sprawled as low as he'd felt that day. He'd gnawed at whether to tell his friend what he knew or not.

More people boarded the bus. In his periphery, Connor saw them consider his seat but move on. Maybe catching sight of his mood in his face.

He'd been leaning toward keeping his mouth shut when Daw had plopped down on the couch beside him, popping open a can a beer. "What's going on in your head?"

"Nothing."

"Not nothing," his friend had countered. "Be honest with me, Connor."

"Be honest with me, Connor." His little sister had asked the same thing. He'd lied then. It hadn't gone well. So this time he went with the truth.

"Okay, fine. But you asked for it. Your girl is trying to trap you into marriage."

Daw's face had blanked.

Then, to his utter surprise, his friend had jabbed a forefinger into his breastbone. "You *fucker*. You never liked her. Are you telling lies to drive a wedge between us? That's plain sad."

Shocked, Connor blurted, "Lies? I heard her practically say it!"

"I believe you heard *something*," Daw sneered. "But you twisted it all out of proportion. Maybe you're paranoid, maybe you're just jealous that I love her more than you. Either way, you're pathetic."

His righteous anger had imploded, leaving him shaking and uncertain. Once, he'd told a lie for all the right reasons, and it had gone wrong. Had he told the truth for all the wrong reasons?

Either way, it had still gone wrong.

And when the girlfriend didn't get pregnant, the rest of the band believed Daw.

The bus's door swung shut and its engine started up. Connor straightened in his seat, jaw tight.

The incident had left him shrewder—he'd never be that clueless again. But it had also shaken him, how easy it was to lose another's faith.

How easy it was to lose even a friend's faith.

No, best not to say anything to Shivawn.

But he'd definitely keep alert.

*   *   *

Shivawn clamped the fiddle under her jaw so hard she was a bit surprised neither wood nor bone broke. Da insisted on daily rehearsals while they were together, whether they had a performance that night or not. He also insisted on practicing full-volume—normally a problem mid-morning in a crowded hotel. Fortunately, Rusty had negotiated with the management, not only for a block of rooms, but for complete and exclusive access to the meeting rooms for practice.

"'Drowsy Maggie' from the top—using Granda's ornamentation, Siobhán. Get it right this time."

"Yes, Da."

She concentrated on the music. Da had taught her the cuts, taps, and trebles just this week, more extensive than Nan's version, which she'd learned at age nine. Da was Shivawn's first fiddle teacher. Though she'd grown up mostly in the US, her father had her a month each summer. Sometimes he'd even come to the States to visit, usually as part of a céilí band tour, and each time, there'd be a fiddle lesson.

That first summer, he'd pressed the instrument into her small hands. "This was my own mam's fiddle, Siobhán. 'Tis the dearest gift I can ever give you. When you play it right, Mam's smile will light Heaven itself. Do her proud or I'll paddle your behind." He'd taught her music, layered heavily with family loyalty and family pride. Tradition. All he'd missed was a song about it.

Shivawn couldn't see it—couldn't picture having a child of her own, putting a fiddle or flute in its hand, then banging on and on about the honor and pride of the Kellys along with the eighth notes.

"No, no, no!"

She jumped as Da underscored his displeasure with three raps on his bodhrán. The music dribbled off, ending with a wheeze from Aunt Katie's accordion closing.

He glared at Shivawn. "You're playing the old ornaments. Where is your family honor? Where is your *head?*"

Her head had been wandering, and her family honor was apparently fatally besmirched, whatever that meant. She sighed. "I'll do better, Da."

"You're feckin' right you'll do better. There's a long line of Kellys to uphold. When the Kelly Traditional Céilí Band started, my da was on bodhrán and Mam on fiddle."

Shivawn knew this speech. She could have recited it word for word with him. *"Da passed his bodhrán to me."*

This time he added, "Nan passed her fiddle to my older sister Annie." He stopped, expression darkening.

Aunt Annie had died young. When Shivawn was growing up, nobody said much about her except, *"It was a great tragedy."* She'd always assumed she'd died from some sort of wasting disease. No one played fiddle again until Shivawn had taken it up.

"You have the honor of playing your nan's fiddle. Act like it!"

Shame at the reprimand burned her, followed by a searing flash of anger. *I'm not a child anymore.* Darn it, she could be a hundred and two and her da's lectures would still hit her ears as scoldings...which was rather funny, when she thought about it. A hundred-and-two-year-old child. In the end, she just gave him a good-natured, "Yes, Da."

They started from the top. The current incarnation of the Kelly Traditional Céilí Band had Da on bodhrán, Shivawn on fiddle, Cousin Margaret on flute, Cousin Liam on mandolin, Aunt Katie (married to a Clancy, but still a feckin' Kelly) on accordion, and Uncle Seamus on hammered dulcimer.

"No, no, no!" Da stopped them again.

Shivawn automatically cringed—until Da went on.

"Seamus, you've got the force of a gnat passing gas. Play that feckin' thing louder, will you?"

"I'm playing as loud as I can, Paddy." In his distress, Seamus forgot to use his American accent, and his Irish came through loud and clear.

"Da," Shivawn began. "If it's too soft, we can hook it up to an amplifier—"

"Siobhán Ó Dubhda Kelly." He turned his snarl on her. "You know better than that."

She did. She also knew what came next, some variation on, *"No amplifyin'!!"* including the double exclamation points.

"We're not amplifyin' the hammered dulcimer! Or the mandolin or *any* instruments. Fancy amps aren't the way *Kellys* make music."

Maybe I'll be an adult by the time I'm a hundred and three. She answered the only way she could, a semi-patient, "Yes, Da."

"Where's your loyalty? You're a Kelly, for feck's sake."

Irritation battled back. "Yes, Da."

"Tradition guides us. Shapes our music. Shapes *us*."

She opened her mouth to chime a third time, *"Yes, Da."*

But darn it, she *was* an adult. More, Connor's music had made an impression on her. *We could do some of that, too.* She dared, "Amplification wouldn't change our sound, though. Only balance the softer instruments with the louder—"

"*Siobhán.*"

He'd shouted in that tone of voice only a parent could manage, a horrified, furious, and terribly, *terribly* disappointed rasp that shrank her soul and reduced her to a shamed little girl.

"Family *supports* each other," Da snarled. "Family *honors* each other."

Adult righteous anger and even humor peeled back to the utter misery of disappointing her father, fueled by a girlhood of vague guilt at her mother's defection. It triggered habitual obedience, trying to make up for it. She managed a barely audible, "Y-yes, Da."

"Now. 'Drowsy Maggie,' from the top."

* * *

That evening, Shivawn mounted the main stage, just abandoned by The Beachies, as the Northwest Punk Express played on the second stage. She stood there, gazing out into the darkened bar. Shadowy, but it would be worse when the stage lights came on, their hard brightness as effective as any wall, like driving into high beam headlights. Then all she'd be able to do was squint and use her peripheral vision.

If she'd thought the place crowded before, tonight was twice as packed.

And upstairs were the three judges.

As the punk band finished, the house lights went up. Rusty mounted the stage beside Paddy Kelly.

"That was our first bracket." She pointed to her right, where a huge tree diagram hung on the upper wall, the names of twenty bands lined up neatly along the left margin, ten empty lines on the right. "As each pair of bands finish, our judges will tell us which goes on to the next round. Let's welcome this year's judges." She applauded to her left, toward the large balcony with a prime view of the dance floor. At the edge sat three people, two men and a woman. "First is Professor Wolfgang Amadeus Laufer, who teaches music theory in Chicago. Professor, what is your vote?"

"Band B had a nice punk rock rhythm." Middle-aged, sandy-haired, and bespectacled, Laufer looked the academic he was. "The lyrics were a bit predictable, however. And the slide-show images projected onto the group as a lighting technique were impossible to see properly, so that was a fail. Band A had a lovely straight-up seventies California style with good technique demonstrated throughout. I pick Band A."

"Band B had a nice, punk rhythm?" barked the other man. " What ivory tower are you living in, Laufer? They were pedaling a load of shit without a wagon."

"Mr. Platt," Rusty drawled. "Please wait for your turn."

Acid spiked in Shivawn's stomach. Hayden Platt was a famous music critic known for his shock reviews. He'd sunk many a fledgling career with his barbed comments. His face was like a lemon in every way—head shape, skin texture, and expression.

"Next, you all know singer Marita Lane. Ms. Lane?"

Shivawn recognized the famous pop singer. Rusty apparently knew the cream of the A-listers.

"I agree, Band A," she said. "Though I think Band B has a vision for their music." She bestowed the sparkling smile that had graced many a platinum album cover on the punk band. "Just follow your unique vision, practice a little more, and you'll be a force to be reckoned with."

Impressive. Not all musicians encouraged each other.

"Thank you, Ms. Lane." Rusty nodded to the singer then turned to the last judge, her mouth tightening slightly before she put on a bright smile. "Our third judge is freelance Chicago music critic, Hayden Platt."

"Band B sucked. Band A couldn't decide whether it was dealing drugs from the sixties or seventies, but at least I could hear the lyrics and understand *some* of them—"

"Thank you, Mr. Platt," Rusty interrupted with a barely hidden glare. "Which do you vote to go to the next round?"

He sat back and crossed his arms. "Band A."

"The Beachies are added to the final playoffs." She pointed at the scoreboard where a large man was already using a long pole to switch The Beachies from the left side to the right. "Are the next two bands ready?"

Showtime. Shivawn's heart gave a frantic pump and began hammering a new rhythm. But instead of a sparkling flutter of anticipation, her pulse beat hard. Too hard. Normally, playing was a rush, but tonight her excitement had an edge to it she didn't like.

Almost like fear.

Then Rusty crowed, "Please welcome the Kelly Traditional Céilí Band!"

Not ready, not ready. Adrenaline hit Shivawn like ice water. The house lights went down, the spotlight flicked on. She clamped her fiddle under her jaw and wiped her hand on her slacks as Da announced their first number. Her hand left an uncharacteristic cool streak, perspiration. Darn it, she hoped she hadn't wet her strings.

Da started before she was ready. She barely got bow to string in time, and her first note *skreeked.* Shivawn winced with mortification. She could *feel* the judges, the weight of their criticism. Worse, her ears rang with the memory of practice this morning. *"Get it right this time, Siobhán."*

Concentrate. Concentrate on getting it right.

But the more she focused on the notes, the less energy she spent on the music.

Worse, the opening song was "Drowsy Maggie." Without her head full in the music, she kept cutting and sliding in the old places.

She told herself it sounded okay. Only the band knew, and they were too professional to react.

But Da would yell at her after.

Her stomach, already queasy, tightened.

The song seemed to go on forever. Her playing should have been light and lively, like dancing along a river's stepping stones. But if the notes were stones, she'd already slipped off a couple times. Now, her pants legs sopping, she less danced from note to note than squished.

After a small eternity, "Drowsy Maggie" ended. Somehow, Shivawn managed to finish the other two songs in the set, clamping down on the horror of that first disaster. But her playing was mechanical, her mind fixated on every minuscule wrong note in the reel.

By the time she left the stage, she was shaking. She tottered back to the cases room to put away her instrument, only half-listening to their rival band. It turned out Windy City's Eagle's Wings was neither Gospel nor country, but a local pop rock band.

The routine act of wiping down her fiddle and loosening the bow hair calmed her. Feeling steadier, she returned to the main room in time to hear their last number. Their beat was good, but the singer was a little weak.

Something Marita Lane gently pointed out. "Band A's crooner gave a good tug on the heartstrings, but Band B's singer was a bit too rough for pop."

As she spoke, Maggie hooked arms with Shivawn and led her toward the bar. "I'd have said he gargled gravel."

Shivawn smiled, and her stomach settled. They'd nailed their other two pieces. Surely a few alternate ornaments would pass notice?

Then Judge Platt harrumphed. "Well, I didn't particularly enjoy either of them. Now, all due respect to Ms. Lane—though without her auto-tuner, she probably couldn't hit middle C the same way three times running."

Finding two empty seats, Shivawn slid onto one while her cousin sat on the other. Shivawn started to signal for the bartender when…

"But that fiddle player," Platt sneered.

Her hand froze.

"Band A's fiddler couldn't cut construction paper, much less the right notes."

Her breath wheezed out. If he'd punched her in the gut it couldn't have hurt worse. *Fiddler…couldn't cut construction paper.*

"Honestly, it sounded like everyone else was playing a Beethoven symphony while she sawed out 'Mary Had a Little Lamb.'"

Shivawn's body went cold. His criticism was a man-size icicle driven straight through her heart. A hailstorm of shame pelted her. *Couldn't cut construction paper.* Platt's slam resonated inside her, getting louder and louder. She reeled from it like an actual hit to the gut.

In her periphery, a dark shadow moved. She glanced over.

It was Connor, and from his scowl, he was not happy.

Oh, no. Will he criticize me too? Platt's words were icicles but Connor was a playing musician, like her. His condemnation would carve her to ribbons.

When he turned his grimace toward her, she wanted to weep.

Chapter Five

Shivawn cringed in anticipation of the whip of Connor's words. His dark glower was enough to make her heart cry.

Then he jerked his chin at the balcony—and rolled his eyes. Silently letting her know Platt was an ass.

Pain receded. She blinked stinging eyes as he miraculously found an empty seat just a few feet away. Somehow, just with him near she felt better. Not great, but better.

"Stay away from that eejit boy."

Not right now, Da.

Nasty McNastypants, also known as Judge Platt, went on. "Their accordion sounded like my wheezing grandma. And the dulcimer player would've made a better sound using those mallets on his skull. Frankly, it's only their singer who redeems them. But, then again, there was nothing redeeming about Band B's singer, who sounded like a pair of skeletons screwing on a tin roof—"

"Band A goes on to the next round," Rusty called out with a black glare at the balcony.

Somehow, miraculously, the man with the pole was pushing the Kelly Traditional Céilí Band nameplate to the right, where it claimed another of the ten winning spots. *No thanks to me.*

Rusty went on, "Next we have…"

As she announced the next bracket, Bartender Ben slid a big mug of ale in front of Shivawn. "On the house."

"Yeah." Normally, she tried to moderate her alcohol when performing. But that brutal beating, verbal though it was, had left her bruised and bleeding; she grabbed the mug and downed it in a few long swallows. "Thanks."

"How dare he?" Aunt Katie squeezed into the spot between Shivawn and the woman in the next stool, any concept of personal space ignored. "*Wheezing?* My accordion is a classic."

"At least we won our bracket." Uncle Seamus gave her a wan smile. "We'll go on to the finals. Despite what that judge said about us. About some of us." His smile slipped.

Poor Uncle Seamus. The *mallets on his skull* comment had to be at least as hurtful as *can't cut paper.* Shivawn plunked down her mug, the fire of anger beginning to war with her shame. They'd won a berth in the next round, but not without paying a painful price. She glared up at Platt, sitting smug in the balcony. Ruining already-fragile egos just because it was entertaining.

"That Platt's an idiot." Cousin Margaret was working on her own tall glass of something colored poison green. "You know what they say?"

"No, what?" She plunked down her empty mug.

"Those who can, do. Those who can't, are critics."

Shivawn laughed, then sobered slowly. "But he had a point. I flubbed 'Drowsy Maggie.' In fact…" She pushed herself to her feet. "I think I'll go back to my room and work on it." *And maybe cry my eyes out.*

"Not yet, young lady." Da steamed toward her. "We are all sitting right here and listening to the competition."

A sick feeling rose in Shivawn's stomach. *Here it comes. The bawling out to end all bawlings out.*

Paddy Kelly glared at the non-Kelly occupants of the stools around Shivawn and Maggie. Most quickly vacated.

Connor subtly shifted down a couple seats.

Shivawn subsided onto her stool, wishing she'd gotten out of there before Da stopped her. All she wanted to do was climb into a hole and disappear.

But instead of bawling her out, Da only sat beside her, seething with condemnation. In a way, it was worse than if he'd simply gotten it over with and yelled.

She'd been criticized before. Hell, she'd even been booed off the stage. Hadn't hurt as bad as this—because in this case, her da and the ass in the balcony *were right*. At least, the scared little kid inside her thought so.

She held up a couple cold fingers. Da wanted her to stay and endure the ice of his silent condemnation? Fine. She'd stay. But she didn't have to do it sober.

Ben came over. "Two mugs?"

"Two pitchers." She waved at the rest of the Kellys. "Six mugs."

Six mugs, though she noted most of the pitchers were drunk by her and Uncle Seamus. His scared inner child must've been hurting as bad as hers.

*   *   *

Connor's heart ached for Shivawn, knowing she was hurting. But when she'd had been up on that stage playing, his jaw had dropped slightly more with each note.

Yeah, maybe she didn't think she was playing well, but her music dazzled him. She interlocked perfectly with the others in the group. Her stage presence was incredible, teasing, then bewitching the audience to rejoice in the music with her. Her fiddle was alternately a solo voice then reinforced and buttressed the others' music.

Somehow, she did it all.

He'd applauded Shivawn so enthusiastically when the Kelly band finished, his own group gave him a dirty look. All except his friend Zach, who startled then stared at Connor thoughtfully.

There went that secret.

Then that tiny-tooled Platt opened his foul mouth.

Connor was furious. He gripped his beer glass harder. He'd respected Shivawn's wishes and stayed away. But she needed him tonight; he knew it.

Oh, her face hadn't shown a jot of how those words knifed her—but the tiny flinches as Platt's words hit, the way her small hand fisted at her side, had shouted it to him.

He wanted to go to her, wrap her in his arms and hold her until those lying, hurtful words had no more power for her. Be her bulwark against that damned Platt.

Connor's gaze shifted to the old man beside her. He wanted to do what her father should have been doing. But because the man was glaring at him, he couldn't, though he suspected said father was the cause of the injunction in the first place.

Didn't matter who was keeping them apart—her father or her—it all boiled down to the fact that Connor was furious, with no place to vent that fury.

He was angry with the judge who'd trashed her feelings. Angrier with *himself*, because his hands were tied, with his own honor doing the tying. *Fucking honor.* He'd respected her wishes, but he wanted desperately to ignore that, ignore everything, and sweep her away.

Unfortunately, he couldn't hug her and make everything all right as he longed to do. Hell, he couldn't even be *with* her—until she was ready for it.

But it was eating him up inside. So he'd found a place near her at the bar—near but not too near for the black glares of Paddy Kelly—and leaned out where she could see. To let her know at least one person thought—no, *knew*—Platt was full of shit, and she was the most wonderful musician there was.

* * *

Judge Platt continued to be an ass. His hateful words resonated in Shivawn's psyche, bleeding from shame...but now beginning to boil with fury, too.

The only thing that kept her from either marching out or slinking out was Da's black glares—and Connor's warm, supportive presence a few feet away.

She had only to turn her head slightly and see his handsome profile to realize life wasn't that bad.

Then the judge would make some asshat remark, and she'd be angry and ashamed all over again. Worse, Platt was so caustic and mean, he often intimidated one of the other judges to vote with him.

As Shivawn ordered a third pitcher of beer, Swingin' from the Chandelier, a forties big band, finished. Almost immediately on the second stage, the familiar lyrics "Hey Jude" began.

She recognized The Battre, the Beatles tribute band she'd met that morning—with the guitarist who'd given her that strange stare. The memory of that dark stare shivered through her, and she tried to douse it with several swallows of beer. Only partially successful. The guy's stare out into the audience now was as robotic as his hammered-out block chords. As soulless. She shivered again and poured everyone another glass, including herself.

The alcohol began to relax her, enough that she could almost enjoy the music. The singer had a pure tone, lending an innocence to the lyrics, and the drummer was rock solid. The band was actually pretty darn good, if she ignored the clang-clang-clang of the rhythm guitar. She finished her glass through the next two songs.

By the time the house lights came up, she'd developed a comfortable buzz. Any shame at her playing or discomfort over the guitarist receded. A decided improvement. She poured another round.

Rusty leaped onto the stage. "Professor Laufer?"

"Band A's take on the swing band was outrageously fresh—awesome lyrics! Band B had a decent cover of those Beatles tunes, but they presented none of the Beatles' style or complexity. I'm definitely going with Band A."

Marita Lane began, "I agree—"

"Not on your life." Platt barged in. "You're completely wrong, Laufer. The style of Band B was pure and perfect. Band A's 'fresh take' was nothing more than a farce! Band

B is clearly the better, and in my opinion deserves to win this whole sorry excuse for a musical showcase."

The singer shut her mouth, expression appalled.

Shivawn plunked down her mug, sloshing out beer and earning a scowl from Da, but she was irritated for Marita Lane's sake. Platt was not only rude, he was a meanie-head.

Rusty cleared her throat into the microphone. "So, that's one for Band A, and one for Band B. Ms Lane?"

"Well, I...um, I'll vote for Band B."

Irritation died to dismay. While audiences went along with the most forceful personality in the group, she'd forgotten the judges could also be swayed.

She started to pour herself a top-off of liquid courage when she noticed Connor unfolding from his barstool. Shivawn tensed up, hand clutching the pitcher handle, belly cold.

He's leaving?

His mere presence had helped her. Sure, having the rest of her family surrounding her was nice—except for Cousin Liam, who'd gotten out before Da came. Still, somehow even all her family wasn't the bolstering presence the bass player was becoming. How could a man she'd barely spoken with have such a large presence in her thoughts?

Then she realized he *had* talked to her—through his music. Talk which went straight to the heart, bypassing silly things like time and space and rational thought.

Which, come to think of it, might be Da's problem with him.

Connor, still honoring her ban on meeting, didn't speak as he passed her. She sucked up her maturity and reluctantly prepared to deal with the pain alone.

But then he half-turned with a gentle smile and a thumbs up.

And suddenly her whole mood changed. Sure, the music critic didn't like her fiddle technique, but who was he? A washed-out journalism major who'd never held an instrument in his life, much less a tune.

Connor was a bona fide performer, and a good one at that. His encouragement proved she'd done okay.

Da, in the stool beside her and already scowling like a thundercloud, actually growled at Connor's back. "What did that boy just do?"

She hid the smile she couldn't stop with another sip. "Nothing, Da."

"He'd better not. Feck it, while we wait for the next bracket, I have a few words for you all about that disaster of a set we had." He tossed off his mug and set it on the bar with a slam.

Her smile faded. She loved playing with the band, but the egos and tempers got a bit much at times. Apparently, Da had been working up to a good lecture. The beer had helped anesthetize her before, so she signaled for a refill from a bartender, not Mr. Sexy but one of the others, so as not to set Da off even more.

Maggie obviously saw the storm brewing in Da's eyes and attempted to disrupt the Kelly hurricane with, "What's Judge Platt's problem, anyway?"

"Who knows?" Aunt Katie rolled her eyes.

"I do." Da stabbed a finger at his sister. "The problem was your playing."

Aunt Katie just glared back—the siblings had been brawling since their first words. A mulish expression grew on her face. "I don't think that's his only problem, Paddy."

Her return only fired Da's temper hotter as his finger jabbed at Shivawn, accusing. "And *you*."

She blanched but was pleased to note her chill of shame was muted this time.

"What the feck is wrong with you? You haven't stunk that bad since you wore diapers."

A beery anger rose inside, but she barely managed to stop from lashing out. It hadn't worked when Aunt Katie did it, and it wouldn't help now. She managed a stilted, "Sorry, Da."

"That's it?" he snarled. "That's all you have to say for yourself? *Sorry?*" His face went bright red as he turned to his next victim. "And what about you, Seamus Clancy?"

"M-me?" Uncle Seamus cringed.

"You heard that music critic. You stunk worse than manky shite." He poked the green-vested chest with a thud. "Feckin' horrid, you were, you useless sod."

Poor Uncle Seamus completely wilted at the vitriol in Da's voice. His glass lowered slowly to the bar, as if it was too heavy for his hand. "You'll want me to quit the band, then."

Horrified, Shivawn spoke up, "No, Uncle Seamus, of course he doesn't—"

"That might be best," Da interrupted.

"What?" She spun toward her da, a man she thought she knew. "Family comes first! Loyalty to the band—"

"Loyalty, yes," he spat. "'Tis loyalty that lets Seamus know the band is better off without him."

Her uncle's fingers slid from his glass. He heaved himself off his stool and slunk away. The crowd swallowed him a moment later.

"Go after him," she cried. "Take it back! Don't you see what you've done to him?"

"He'll get over it."

She stared at her da. She'd seen him angry before, but never so severe. It shocked her. Scared her.

And then, thinking of how destroyed Uncle Seamus looked, and after all Da drummed into her how family *supported* each other, anger plumed inside her, a sudden volcano of righteous fire.

All the times her suggestions, and those of Cousin Maggie or Cousin Liam, were treated as dirt, because that wasn't the way *Kellys* made music. All the times Da had thrown his weight around...

She had stayed with the band out of family loyalty. And now it turned out family loyalty was a crock of shite.

Chapter Six

"The rest of you." Da turned his scowl on Aunt Katie and Cousin Margaret. "Rehearsal tomorrow morning at eight. No excuses."

Maggie's cheeks stained with embarrassment. Aunt Katie took her revenge by ordering herself up a Kilbeggan whiskey, neat, three fingers, and when the bartender named the price, she pointed at Da.

Da sat with his arms tightly folded, jaw jutting, a sure sign of righteous anger.

Shivawn's own fury burned hotter. Didn't he even care he was treating them like naughty children? Didn't he care how he made poor Uncle Seamus feel?

She almost got up then and stomped off. She'd even slapped down her mug with a satisfying thud of indignation when Rusty took the spotlight.

"The last pairing of the night," the country legend announced. "Levan Polkka and—" she threw her hand toward the band behind her, "—Taboo Soul."

Shivawn's heart immediately beat harder. Any thoughts of leaving disappeared.

Just seeing Connor onstage made her forget her da, her anger, her shame. As the band played, his bass line was a bedrock, the solid foundation for the rest's pyrotechnics. The kind of unquestioning support a family was supposed to give...

Honestly, how can Da think this music is lesser, in any way?

As he'd done before, Connor began driving the music forward—driving the audience with it. The listeners probably thought they were electrified by the soaring voice of the lead singer; the dancers likely felt they were energized by the fiery fretwork of the lead guitar.

She knew different. In reality, it was Connor's exceptional musicianship and relentless bass which brought the set to a roaring climax.

Shivawn leaped to her feet to applaud his daring, brilliant musicianship—and reeled, nearly falling. She grabbed her stool, swaying drunkenly.

How much beer have I had?

Around her, the crowd's cheering nearly drowned out the last chord hits.

Connor's amazing, glorious music—she *wanted* that. She wanted bass notes low enough to shake the foundation of her being. Loud enough to electrify her whole body. Oh, to spin a reel driven by the force of a true bass, one she could not just hear but *feel* because it rattled her bones. Energized by the crash of cymbal and snap of snare from a real drum set, not the thump of a bodhrán. Inspired by the strut of an electric guitar, not the wheeze of a second-hand accordion, and oh heavens, not the barely heard plink-plunk of an unamplified hammered dulcimer.

She wanted dazzling, earth-shaking music. Music she'd *never* get because Da never electrified anything.

Unless I play with Connor.

Excitement splashed inside her at the thought.

Squashed just as quick by Da's growl. "What do you think you're doing, Siobhán? We don't cheer our enemies."

She slid back onto her stool, shoulders folded tight, chest cold and dark. *Play with Connor, right.* The bassist was forbidden—forbidden by Da, with his they're-the-enemy, family-first rhetoric.

Meaningless bullshit.

But if Da doesn't have to follow his own damned rules, why do I?

She straightened her spine, blinking in profound amazement at the stage. *I don't.*

A new tidal wave of excitement built at the realization, rolling over her and leaving her breathless. Connor had wanted to connect with her. If he still did, all she had to do was talk with him.

But she wasn't an idiot. Meeting him anywhere public, that was, under Da's scrutiny, wouldn't do. She needed somewhere private, like her hotel room.

Only, Maggie was there. Unless...

Shivawn tapped her chin thoughtfully, missing her face the first time. Maybe Country Boys and Cowboy Boots had optimistically booked their rooms for the whole week, and her cousin would be otherwise occupied.

"Maggie," she began. "About tonight. Are you and..."

Da cleared his throat, and she glanced over to see him staring at her, his eyes narrow like a knife. Her words dribbled off.

Even her hotel room wouldn't be private if Da thought she was bringing any *eejit boys* up.

"What about tonight?" Maggie asked.

"Are you...are you wanting more beer?" Brightly, she picked up the pitcher and sloshed the remainder into Cousin Margaret's glass—well, mostly into her glass. The bartender *tsked* and brought out a dishcloth.

Maggie eyed her almost as narrowly as Da.

Behind them, Levan Polkka started their set. Singers only, an *a cappella* group from the Baltics. They were wonderful, but couldn't compete with the sheer raw power of Taboo Soul.

Maggie's penetrating look cleared to comprehension, and she nudged Shivawn. "Did you hear? The diner has a special on *Footlongs* tonight. All night." Then she actually winked.

It took a moment for Shivawn to remember Maggie's nickname for the lead singer of Country Boys and Cowboy Boots was Footlong. Not only had her cousin just told her what she was doing tonight, she'd implied she'd be gone *all* night. Leaving Shivawn the room to herself. Or—if she was bold enough—leaving the room to herself and one very special electric bass player. Excitement dumped bright and sharp into her stomach.

As the last band wrapped up, she was nervous enough to chew nails, but her excitement grew as Connor's band was picked in a rare unanimous vote by the judges.

She could make music with Connor—if she was brave enough to invite him to her room.

Taboo Soul versus Levan Polkka was the last bracket of the evening. Released from listening to the competition for tonight, Shivawn hopped down from her stool—and nearly face-planted. Grabbing the rail, she waited until the room stopped spinning. Yeah, she was drunk all right. Which made her question her decision. How much of wanting to meet with Connor was true musical desire, and how much was just fermented courage? Maybe she should go back to the hotel and sleep it off instead.

Carefully, she released her grip, concentrating fiercely on staying upright. Her legs were strangely wobbly as she tottered toward the back room where the cases were stored. Last minute, she detoured into the ladies' room for a comfort stop.

After washing her hands, she scooped a few mouthfuls of water to try to dilute the alcohol in her bloodstream. Cooler and a bit steadier, she collected her fiddle under the eagle eye of a mountain of a guy with a thick neck and boxer's muscles. Even drunk, she could tell no instruments were walking away with him there.

Only one of the three buses waited at the curb. Apparently, she'd been slower than she thought—or in her drunken state, time was blurrier. On board, when the bus lurched into motion, she had to grab her fiddle case to her middle to steady herself, and she closed her eyes to keep her head from spinning. *Blurrier, then.*

Minutes later the bus pulled up in front of the hotel. She reeled inside. The first thing she saw was the open archway into the hotel bar, the musicians inside either drowning their sorrows or raising celebratory glasses.

Including the singer and lead guitarist from Taboo Soul.

Shivawn stopped. Stomach and thoughts churning, she stared at the two, not knowing if she wanted to find Connor with them or not. She gripped the handle of her case harder.

Yes, she'd wanted to invite him to jam—but while drunk and angry and not thinking straight. The consequences... Even if all they did was play a few tunes, making music with Connor could never be meaningless. And if Da found out, there'd be hell to pay.

Her heart urged her to ignore reason, to go into the bar, find Connor, and take him up to her room. A little shiver ran through her at the thought of her and him, in a bedroom, alone.

But finding trouble was one thing. Seeking it out was something else. Being rash in the heat of the moment, maybe she'd have done it. Being intentionally rash held no appeal.

Sighing, she pushed herself back into motion, shuffling past the celebrating groups toward the elevator which would take her to her floor. She'd go to her room, alone.

Where she'd practice, alone. Sleep, alone.

Poor Shivawn.

Feeling extravagantly sorry for herself, she turned the final corner to the elevator...

Her stomach dropped, and she lurched to a stop and stared.

Connor waited beside the closed doors, the up arrow already lit. Big, handsome, and a little sad looking. She wondered what put the blues in his dark gaze.

A battle set up inside her. Sanity pushed her to lurch wordlessly past him and take the stairs. Anger with Da urged her to grab his wrist with her free hand and drag him to her room.

But that sadness in his gaze...compassion won out over everything else.

Shivawn padded up beside him and set down her case. "What's wrong?"

He spun, surprise replacing the sorrow. Then, as he recognized her, something more lit his eyes, something that looked like...joy.

"You're talking to me, now?"

She managed a small smile. "Probably something I'll regret."

He grinned at that, and something in her heart lightened. "So, what's wrong?"

"Oh." He heaved a sigh. "I was just thinking about tonight. How harsh it was, not just for the losers. There will be a lot of emotionally hobbled music and musicians, courtesy of Judge Platt." His gaze went distant and sorrowful.

"Yeah." She found herself wanting to soothe that sad look...by caressing his face. She stuffed her hands in her pockets. "If it's any consolation, I caught Rusty's expression as she marched up to the judges' lounge. There may be a second annual Battle of the Bands, but I don't think Platt will be part of it. We can't figure out what that guy's deal is."

Connor's gaze came back to her, and he barked a laugh. "Can't you tell? He hates anything that's not pure. Pure metal, pure blues—but especially, pure sixties rock and roll." He gave a quick, disgusted snort. "Know what I think? He popped his cherry to the Beatles."

She thought she'd never laugh again, but that did it. "Nailed it."

As she laughed, Connor joined in, freely, his eyes crinkled. Laughing with Connor, the joke seemed funnier, richer...until she realized what she was doing. Her laughter died, leaving her simply staring at him.

Hungrily.

Connor's laughter faded, his gaze locked on hers. A question in them...and a hope.

Shivawn's heart soared. She had an empty room for music—with an equally empty set of beds.

"Stay away from that eejit boy."

Satisfying either hunger would have a price.

And who's life is it? Da's, or mine?

Tonight her father had stifled her, insulted Aunt Katie, and nearly crippled Uncle Seamus. Her fury returned.

Enough is enough.

She firmed her posture. "Connor, I have to check on my uncle. Da said something to him...well, I need to make sure he's okay. But then..." When it came down to it, she felt suddenly shy. Her gaze dropped to where his chest rose and fell with a comfortable rhythm. "Then, would you like to join me...in my room? To make music," she hastened to add.

His chest froze abruptly. Then it pummeled faster.

Her gaze rose to his.

The fire in his eyes burned her from the inside out.

He answered in one word.

"Yes."

Chapter Seven

Shivawn checked on Uncle Seamus and found him philosophical but steady, and not nearly as broken as she'd feared. An open book rested spine up on the corner chair, a paper cup and bottle of wine on the stand beside it. He unwrapped another paper cup and poured her some sparkling water.

"Your da needed a scapegoat, Shivawn. His whole being is wrapped up in the band, you know."

She snorted as she set down her fiddle case and accepted the cup. "His ego is, certainly."

Seamus waved her to sit at the small dining table. "More than that. That band...it's how he honors his parents."

"I don't understand?" She'd heard Granda this and Mam that, but never why. She eased into the chair across from her uncle and sipped sparkling water.

"Honoring their tradition is how he shows his love for them. But more, it's how he passes their love to you, to me, to the rest of his family."

She blinked, her arm slowly dropping. When the paper cup hit the table with a *chock*, she rallied. "That doesn't excuse how he treated you."

"Be kind, Shivawn." He patted her hand where it rested on the cup. "His loyalty to family is what causes him to be harsh."

"Then where's his loyalty to you?" She underscored it with a slash of her free hand. "He kicked you out!"

"That was just his temper talking." Uncle Seamus gave her a wan smile. "He felt he'd failed us with that set, and he needed a safe way to vent his distress. I'm happy to do that for him. You mark my words. Once he calms down, it'll be like nothing happened."

She was confused, angrier for Seamus than he was for himself. "At the very least, he owes you a big apology."

"Does the storm apologize? No, it rains furiously for all of a night, then the next morning has cleared to sunshine." He pushed back his chair and rose. "Thank you for stopping by, Shivawn. But I'll be fine, and tomorrow he'll be fine, too."

She snatched up her fiddle case and left frustrated and unsure, stalking to the elevator where she fumed and fussed for several minutes without hitting the button.

Da shouldn't be allowed to treat Uncle Seamus like that.

Her uncle was too kind-hearted and forgiving. But how to get that fact through Da's thick skull? A hit upside the head with a foam clue bat? Spank the smart into him? Give him an open mind with the Meat Cleaver of Understanding...?

Her alcohol-tinged thoughts had become not just unhelpful, but ridiculous. She smiled slightly at herself and pressed the up button. Above the elevator doors, the indicator for four was lit.

Both Da and Uncle were adults—in the end, they'd have to work it out for themselves. For now, she deliberately turned her thoughts away from the rat hole she'd made of the issue.

Connor filled her mind, and she smiled.

She'd made contact with him and it was glorious. Joy lifted her onto her toes. And now she'd make music with him, and that would be glorious, too. She took a fresh grip on her fiddle-case handle and waited.

And waited.

The floor light never changed. The elevator stayed stalled on four.

Oh, what the heck. It was only three floors, and she was too excited to stand there.

Heart light, Shivawn ran up the stairs. She'd given Connor her room number before they'd parted. Maybe he'd even be waiting for her there, outside her room.

She'd let him in. They'd jam. Maybe talk. Maybe more...

She opened the stairwell door onto her floor and stopped cold, chest deflating.

The hallway was empty.

*   *   *

Connor, after watching Shivawn leave the elevator on the second floor for her uncle's room, rode the car to three, where he stopped to brush his teeth and take a quick swipe with a washcloth.

And to get a couple what-if supplies.

He grinned ruefully at himself as he dug the single strip of plastic packages from the bottom of his luggage. While the rest of the band seemed to carry condoms by the roll, his passion had always been the music. Sure, he enjoyed a romp as much as the next person, but it all paled next to letting the music pour out of him, the throbbing bass vibrating through his hands and body and his very soul.

Music had always been his passion—until tonight.

Shivawn.

She was different. He looked forward to simply being with her, so much so that he bypassed the elevator to dash up the stairs. Headed to five-oh-two, to *her* room. Where they'd make music and maybe, much, much more.

Gripping his bass case handle with so much excitement he almost broke it, he threw open the stairwell door to the fifth floor...

A short man stood hunched over one of the doors, head down, as if intent on something.

Or intent on *hiding* something.

"Hey." Connor strode toward the guy. "What are you doing?"

The man's camel-brown head snapped up, revealing he'd been shoving a card at the door. Connor's muscles clenched, seeing the guy's face below a bad bowl haircut. It was the Battre guitarist, the one who'd stared strangely at them at the diner. Who'd stared at *Shivawn.*

He wasn't sure what the guy's problem was, whether he hated all the rival bands or just them, but he didn't like how Mr. Battre had been hunched at the door, even more alarmed when he saw the door number. Five-oh-two. Shivawn's room.

He picked up his pace. "That's not your door."

"N-no?"

The guitarist fell back, blinking uncomprehendingly at him. As if he didn't get it, didn't know what he was doing—

though Connor thought the blinking a bit mechanical, overdone. Suspicious.

Or am I just paranoid? "What's your room number?"

"Four-oh-two."

Four-oh-two, five-oh-two. A reasonable mistake?

Grinding his molars, he stabbed at the elevator. "Your room's down one floor."

"Oh. Right. Thanks." The guitarist grinned uncertainly.

This looked more natural, making Connor question his gut certainty the guitarist had been up to no good. Then, when the guy tried to turn toward the elevator and only managed to stumble over his own feet and face-plant against the wall, Connor felt like a complete ass.

The Battre guy pushed himself upright and started for the elevator.

"Wait. I'll help you." He followed, annoyed at both Mr. Battre and himself. Not sure of anything at the moment except his gut still roiled with suspicion. "What's your name?"

"John Smith. But tha's too 'merican. M'band name's Roger Townshend."

The slurring appeared a bit overdone, too, but since he was making up for his paranoia, he said cheerfully, "Roger Townshend? Like Roger Daltrey and Pete Townshend of The Who?"

"The who?"

"You know. The band, The Who."

"I never heard of The Band."

"Never mind." Much more and it would devolve into an Abbott and Costello routine.

Connor managed to shovel John Smith or Roger Townshend or whoever the hell he was into the elevator, where he pushed the button for the fourth floor. When the car arrived, he helped the guy out, started to follow, then thought of Shivawn. A tug to return instantly to wait for her was so insistent he nearly leaped back on the elevator. But common sense told him she would be a while with her uncle.

Townshend was already at his door, trying to fit the key card in the lock's slot and missing. The elevator had an old-fashioned stop button for unloading freight, so with a sigh, he pulled it out to keep the car ready for him to pop back up to five then joined him.

"Here. Let me." He plucked the card from the drunk man's hand and slid it in. A click and green light later, the door swung open.

Connor stood in the entryway while Townshend stumbled through strewn dirty clothes to the refrigerator. From the discarded piles and crumpled rubbish, it looked like all five Battre band members were staying in the room. Not an outlandish idea. Contrary to public opinion, most bands were barely making a living. They couldn't afford the luxury of individual accommodations.

"Want a drink?" Townshend spun from the mini-fridge with an open green glass bottle in his hand, a big swashy grin on his face. "To cerr-erbate. I mean, celebrate." He started to laugh, hiccupped instead, and slapped his free hand over his face. A giggle escaped anyway.

Connor heaved another sigh. "Don't you think you've had enough?"

"We'z one step closer to a r'cording contract. I'm getting blasted."

"Why aren't you downstairs with your crew getting blasted?"

"This is cheaper. Brung it m'self" He jerked the bottle up, too fast, sloshing some out.

The sting of cheap wine hit Connor's nostrils as rivulets ran down the green glass onto Townshend's hand.

The other guitarist seemed not to notice. "Wanna glass?" He then undermined his offer by drinking directly from the bottle.

"Thanks, no. Have at it, buddy." Connor turned to go.

"Hey, know what'd be fun?" The glug of the guitarist taking a swig was followed by a belch. "Let's take one of those shoo' buses out for a spin."

He stopped short, his shoulders tightening. Without turning, he said, "That's stealing, bud."

"Not if we bring it back. C'mon, it'll be fun."

The smart thing to do, the thing he *wanted* to do, was to leave. He'd gotten Townshend safe to his room, done deal.

But Connor had seen his own friends like this too often. They'd drink themselves blind then if they were lucky, pass out. Conscious, they got into real trouble. He didn't know if Townshend could get his hands on a set of keys or hotwire a bus, but could he live with himself if the guy took another life in a drunk driving accident? Especially if it would be just a few minutes of his time to get him safe in bed.

Connor kneaded the tension from his forehead. "Okay, bud." He picked his way through the clothes into the room, plucked the bottle from the man's hand, and set it aside. "Let's get you to bed."

It took cajoling and patience—and three more times setting the bottle aside—but eventually, he got Townshend's jacket and boots off and the guy under the covers. Then, on second thought, he picked up the boots, took them to the bathroom, and plopped them into the dry tub where he hid them behind the shower curtain. That'd keep the guitarist from wandering out and stealing a bus.

He'd turned out the lights and was just cracking the door when he heard retching sounds from behind him.

Sighing so deep it came from his soul, Connor returned to help the drunk man into the bathroom, just in time.

77

Chapter Eight

Shivawn let herself into her room, still hoping Connor had just stepped away for a moment to answer a call of nature...or to get his practice amp...or extra strings for his bass. Something, *anything*, other than the increasingly likely explanation as the minutes ticked by—that he'd had second thoughts and blown her off.

And not in a good way.

After half an hour of pacing, she threw her hands in the air and pulled her sleep shirt from the drawer. She'd just taken off her makeup and undressed when a knock came at the door. A zing arrowed through her.

Connor.

Probably not. She tried to calm her pounding anticipation. Probably Cousin Margaret returning for supplies or something. Padding to the peephole, she looked out.

Connor is here.

This time the zing of excitement, propelled by the reality of him standing there, impaled her as hard and hot as a spear. Her mouth suddenly wet, she swallowed and opened the door to the width of the slide.

She pressed her face in the gap, making sure to keep her scantily clad self out of sight. "I didn't think you were coming."

He grimaced, gaze on his shoes. "Sorry about that. I was here, but then... One of the guys from The Battre was in a bad way. I had to settle him down."

"Oh." A good reason—or possibly an excuse for second thoughts? She gave him an easy way out, just in case. "Well, it's late."

"Yes." He continued to stare at his shoes.

"I was already in bed." Now, if he didn't want to be here, he'd agree and go. Or would he stay? She held her breath.

"Ah." Still standing there, still not looking at her. Not going, but not asking to stay, either.

Finally she blurted, "Did you want to come in—?"

"I have my guitar," he said at the same time, as he lifted the case and his eyes rose to her.

Joy at his answer was a rosebud of happiness opening warm and full in her chest. "I'll need to dress."

"I'll wait."

Last time he'd agreed to wait, he'd apparently arrived but had been drawn away. She didn't want that happening again, or at least, not because of her. She shut the door and threw on jeans and a T-shirt so fast she got the blue jeans equivalent of rug burn.

But, though she scorched her skin zipping, when she looked out the peephole, the hallway was empty.

Her heart shriveled. She wanted to wail. *Again.*

Then a shadow moved past the telescope view. He was there after all. Pacing.

Could he be as nervous and excited as she was?

Her heart steadied down into a fast, eager rhythm, and it was all she could do not to throw the door open like a demented jack-in-the-box.

Belatedly, she tried for dignity, posed languidly along the door frame, and did her best forties-actress "Hello." Unfortunately, her whooshing heart made it a stuttered, breathless, "H-h-he-llo."

"Hi. Thanks for inviting me."

He strode by her into her room, and two things struck her.

First, his scent, teasing her nose as he passed. Male, and clean. Cleaner than *she* smelled, after that sorry excuse for a winning set.

Second, his size. She was used to Da and Uncle Seamus and Cousin Liam, who were taller than her but not by much. Connor's dark head made the ceiling look much lower, and the way he moved, he filled the suddenly small space.

Or maybe he had just that much presence—and it occurred to her he'd have that much presence in bed, too, covering her with his big body.

A wild shudder hit her at the thought.

Breathing fast, she watched him set down his guitar case and a sturdy-looking practice amp.

Ready to get to the main show already?

Nerves seared her. She wasn't ready for intimacy yet.

But when Connor turned toward her, he only used his now-free hands to gesture at her fiddle case. "Play for me?"

Given the direction her thoughts had been taking, it was unexpected enough that she bleated, "Wh-what?"

"Before we jam." He gave her a tiny smile, as if he knew what she'd been thinking and was telling her he hadn't meant to scare her. "I really love hearing you play with your family, but...well, I'd like to hear the music that's you. Pure you."

"Oh." That was lovely and sweet.

Chest warming with tender feelings, she opened her fiddle case, took out the bow, and twisted its tension screw to tighten its hair. She thought about scuffing on some rosin, but the way her hand was shaking, she'd end up filing the cake into a cloud of dust. Besides, she still had plenty on the bow from the performance.

Picking up her fiddle, she placed the lower bout against her collarbone, tucked the chinrest under her jaw, and put her hand into position around the neck. Her fingers trembled slightly.

Connor noticed. "Are you okay?"

She paused. Fingers trembling, heart beating hard—harder than any performance. *Was* she okay?

When she took up her fiddle to practice, she was focused, practical, and intent on honing her music. When she took it up to perform, it was different. Not only was she excited to share the result of all her hard work with appreciative listeners. With each performance, she put a bit of her heart on display.

But performing for Connor... a listener who was not merely appreciative but understood all the work that went into making it sound easy? Well, this would put her *soul* out there, too.

This was the most intimate thing she'd ever done.

And it felt *right*. So right she nearly wept with it. Instead she simply smiled and, heart full, met his gaze. "Yes. I'm better than okay."

Shivawn brought up the bow with an automatic flourish. The gesture, done so many times over the years, put her immediately in the zone, and she launched into "Cooley's Reel."

She'd played the piece a thousand times, but this night it burned with a special fire. Connor's eyes gleaming, watching her, amplified and inspired her in a way no regular audience could. Listeners might applaud or shout encouragement. Dancers might sway with the beat, letting the music move them. But as a musician, especially as an instrumentalist, he not only lived the music, he created it. Now, he seemed to create it, breathe life into it, *with her.*

As she played the opening phrases, Connor nodded in time...and then he began nodding slightly ahead of the beat, as if urging her to play faster. His easy smile said he was superbly confident that she could.

That smile, that nod, challenged her to dig into the strings, to make them vibrate with an electric energy.

His foot began to tap, his gaze to glow. She played faster, and faster yet, until the fiddle exploded with notes, flowing from her fingers as rapidly and relentlessly as a gully wash. Her music became a flood of joy, sweeping her away.

Sweeping him away, too. His whole body began to pulse with her music, a muscular volley of shoulder and torso that infused the atmosphere with a primitive, sexual throbbing.

Or maybe that was just her.

Just before the end, she stopped abruptly. Connor, somehow completely attuned to her, ceased all movement. She stood there, breathless, gaze locked with him. She put bow to strings and finished the piece off with a slow double-stop slide.

"Fantastic!" Smiling like the sun, he applauded. "Absolutely marvelous. Technically brilliant, emotionally compelling. Plus you're an outstanding showman."

"Thanks." Pleasure buoyed her. "Now, show me yours." Only after she said the words did she hear the innuendo, and she slapped the back of her bow hand over her mouth.

His grin turned wicked. "I thought you'd never ask." He snatched up his case, threw it open on the bed, and lifted out his electric bass, a gorgeous Ibanez.

While he strapped himself in, she laid her violin in its case then plugged his amp into the electrical socket under the room's desk.

"All right." He lay a couple riffs down on the unamplified strings, getting his fingers warmed up. "What key is that song in?"

"It's not a 'song.' It's a *reel*." Only after she snapped the words did she hear the crotchety tone.

Great tap-dancing leprechauns, I sound like Da.

She flashed him an apologetic smile. "Sorry. We play it in E minor."

He nodded.

While he noodled a bit, she added, "There are only two chords. Three, if you want to get complicated."

"E minor and D," he said without looking up. "With G thrown in to be fancy?"

"Why, yes." Startled delight tickled her.

He glanced at her with a grin. "You sound surprised."

"I am. Most players I know learn by rote."

"I'm not most players."

"Yes." Her belly shimmied. "I'm beginning to realize that. How did you know, then?"

"I think in terms of chords. That way, I always have a tonal center when creating the bass line. Or a way to lead into a new key, maybe with a dominant seventh."

"Wow. I've only ever thought of melody and rhythm and beat."

"That's your job, as a melody instrument." With another wicked grin, he plugged the guitar lead into the amplifier's input then fiddled with some controls. "All right, let's turn this bad boy on."

She realized there were not one, not two, but six knobs on the thing. "Why don't you just turn this up?" She touched a fingertip to the master knob.

"This?" He touched the same knob, brushing her finger.

His skin's warmth shivered through to hers. She sucked in a surprised breath, her chest lifting with pleasure.

"It regulates the signal going from amp to speaker." His gaze rose to hers and darkened. He cleared his throat and moved his fingertip to touch the control labeled "Gain." "I also need to make sure there's signal going from my guitar into the amp."

"Ah."

He checked his own volume knobs on the guitar, then walked an experimental riff.

Her ears pricked with delight at the easy, clean run. Her belly warmed and tumbled, fascinated by his long, artistic fingers, not simply for the music coming from them, but also their size and strength and pleasing shape. She searched for words to tell him...but the only phrases that came to her were too intimate too soon, so she settled for a simple, "Cool."

"Wait." He played a slow jazz walking bass, a boo-bop that sounded like *Seinfeld*, one she recognized as "Another

One Bites the Dust," then the early sixties rhythm and blues bass line of "Stand by Me."

As he played, his head bent slightly over the instrument. A lock of black hair fell over his forehead, twisting something in her gut. Unconsciously, she reached out to nudge the lock aside, to touch his silky hair… At the last minute she jerked her hand to the control labeled "Mid" and spun it all the way to the right. "Gorgeous, but what does this do?"

He laughed. "What is it with you and knobs?" He reached for the treble—just as she did.

Their hands collided, his warm, large. Strong. A longer, harder shiver coursed through her.

He caught it, his eyes growing black.

Flustered, she pulled her hand back. "It's just, do these controls make a difference?"

"Oh, yes." His tone was soft, almost breathless.

She hung on his dark gaze, heart beating in her ears…and then he smiled and stepped back.

Knowing she wasn't ready. Giving her space.

She fell a little in love with him at that moment.

"Yes, they make a difference. Listen." He adjusted the treble—then played a regular guitar solo on four strings which would usually take six.

Normally thick, cumbersome bass strings moved like an elephant trying to pirouette. He'd not only made the elephant twirl, he'd turned it into a sleek prima ballerina whipping out fouetté turns. Amazement burned through her like a fuse, combusting into a delighted laugh. "Was that you or the knobs?"

"Me, but without this…" Connor touched the mid, lightly, almost teasingly. "And this." He caressed the treble. "The notes don't speak clearly."

His touch on the knobs was so sweet, so sliding and sensual, that she could almost feel him doing that to her skin. Shuddering with lust, she let out a soft moan.

His gaze rose to hers, hungry. But also patient, waiting for her own hunger to meet—and exceed—his.

Her throat thickened. She swallowed, but it was hard. "Th-that's why you give such a great performance." Her breasts tightened at the idea of him, *performing*. "Onstage, that is."

The hunger in his gaze intensified. "Onstage, I have help. Starstruck's sound system has kickass bass amp stacks."

Need churned inside her at the stark desire in his gaze. "Well, you certainly know how to use *everything* to good effect." She heard the heat in her words, the innuendo, but for the first time didn't care. Her lips felt swollen and throbbed with the need to cool themselves...by pressing them to his.

As if he felt it, too, his gaze dropped to her mouth. Stark need flared in his eyes. Pressing her lips to his right now wouldn't cool them, but set them both on fire.

His gaze rose to hers. A question sat there. *Are you ready?*

Almost.

He read her flawlessly, reaching toward her, and she trembled, anticipating his touch like a diver anticipates the onrushing cold water...

Connor reached past her to flick the knobs back to the middle then grinned at her. "Okay, let's try this, then. You start."

"Wait, what?" She spun mental gears helplessly for a moment, realized he'd read not only her desire but her slight hesitation, and was grateful to him for postponing the physical intimacy in favor of the musical… And then she got it. Her heart lurched then slammed into a new fast rhythm. "You mean, both of us play? I thought you'd play some more first."

"Shivawn." His grin fell away. He stared at her with a fragile, almost vulnerable cast. "I've been looking forward to this since you suggested it. Hoping for it for long before that. Please?"

She'd jammed with other musicians before. But never with such a primal instrument as the electric bass, and never a musician so handsome.

So forbidden.

A dark shiver seized her. "Well…"

"Please?" he repeated, almost a whisper.

Shadowy, barely understood dangers danced in her heart, but the heartfelt plea persuaded her. "Okay. But if it doesn't go well—"

"You just start. I'll catch your tempo."

Dark dangers were banished by his relieved, confident grin. Fresh excitement rat-a-tatted her heart as she retrieved her fiddle from its case and tucked it under her chin, at the precipice of a musical and a relationship cliff. It was all so brand-new. If this worked—or even better, if they soared together—it might lead to so much more.

Or it might crash and burn.

No pressure.

Shivawn started the reel, playing the first four bars alone. On the fifth, Connor hit the tonic.

Exactly in time with her.

That deep, dark note, even on the practice amp, resonated through her from her crown to her toes, rumpling the most sensitive flesh with an excited shiver.

Her fingers kept going, but only because she'd played the tune so often it was ingrained.

He let that bass note vibrate through that bar and the next. Then, as she hit the height of the phrase, he thumbed a D that rang like a bell.

Excitement goosed her. She ran down the rest of the phrase to the start of the next bar, expecting him to hit the D again with her on beat one.

He didn't. Disappointment seared...

Until he played the D on beat *two*, and a slide to E on beat three that she felt as an actual physical slide, silk on naked skin.

She hit the B theme, expecting the walk of a steady four-four, the square foundation her band usually laid for her. But Connor...

His beat two crowded in on beat one, the "and" of the beat pressing tight after. Like a line of people pushing from behind, the effect drove both her and the music forward. By the second time through, she was spinning out notes so fast she was laughing in pure delight. The end was a spontaneous blur of double-stops up and off the end of her fingerboard while he slid all the way to his lowest note and plucked it with such vigor that it shook the whole room.

As the last note rang, she spontaneously reached out to touch his shoulder. "That was *amazing*..." Her fingers came in contact with warm, cotton-covered male muscle, far harder than anything she'd ever felt. Her words dribbled off to nothing but a stare.

His gaze lifted at the touch, fusing to hers, his eyes dilating until they were pure black pools.

The moment sang.

"Again," he rasped.

She didn't know if he meant the song or the touch. Taking the safer alternative, she raised her fiddle and started playing.

He joined her immediately this time, and they played the tune once, meshing so perfectly her whole being thrilled.

And then Connor got cooking.

He started grinding that bass out in a rhythm that made her blood boil, pushing her. She played faster, and faster, and faster yet. Lust and music rushed in her veins.

His gaze held hers, both of them playing to a lather. The fire in Connor's eyes and grin of pure joy on his face told her he was as turned on as she.

The reel was coming to an end, her heart was banging in her chest, and she wanted Connor like she'd never wanted a man before.

They finished the song in a flurry of notes.

She threw the instrument and bow on Maggie's bed—the first time in her life she didn't put the fiddle away in its case—then grabbed Connor's guitar strap and tried to wrestle him out of his bass while he struggled to turn it off and unplug it. And then he was helping her relieve him of his instrument, thrown on the bed beside hers. She drove hands into his hair to pull his mouth to hers, but he was already there, pressing lips against her, mouth open and questing. The kiss was hot and steamy with lots of driving tongue, hers and his, thrusting in the rhythm of the music, still in her head.

She wrenched on the hem of his shirt as he tore off hers. Hands made strong and callused by hours of practice ran over her skin, leaving thrills and goosebumps of pleasure in their wake and driving her to grab great handfuls of hot male muscle in return. Clothes fell as quickly as he could get them off her. She was as eager or more stripping him.

She pressed against him, naked flesh to naked flesh, her breasts flattening uncomfortably against his chest because her nipples were painfully erect. When he grabbed her thighs and lifted, she wrapped legs around strong, perfect hips as he carried her to bed.

Perfect. Their music together was perfect, and their lovemaking just as perfect. Driving rhythm and tight harmony pushed to a brilliant climax, leaving peace in its wake.

"Shivawn," he whispered. "That was..." He took her hand and put it on his chest, and opened his own on her breastbone.

Connecting. Heart to heart. She smiled.

She fell asleep in his arms, her head pillowed on his chest, listening to the beat of his heart, as steady and perfect as his music.

Shivawn dreamed of Da yelling at her, *"You stay away from that eejit boy,"* and she woke in a panic...until a hand reassuringly caressed her hair.

Connor. She raised her gaze to find his on her, soft and loving. Her muscles relaxed slightly.

"Bad dream?" he asked.

"Cautionary. My da...he can't find out about this."

"Our...jamming?" He gave her a faint smile.

"That, too." She placed a hand over his heart. "I'm serious, Connor. He told me no consorting with the enemy. If he finds out, there'll be hell to pay."

"The enemy." He sighed, but his stroking hand was soothing. "Don't worry, Shivawn. He won't find out from me."

She relaxed fully in his arms, laying her head on his chest. Yes, she'd blown staying away from Connor, but that didn't mean it would end in disaster. There was no reason Da had to find out.

The more she thought about it, the more she liked the idea.

This—us—can't be wrong. We're so natural together.

It was almost as if it was meant to be, with how perfectly they'd meshed. Surely fate wouldn't put them together, let them experience this wonder, then snatch it away?

She didn't know where this was going, or if they had any kind of future. But abandoning this amazing passion simply to placate her da and his prejudices was wrong.

Besides. *She* wasn't going to tell Da. *Connor* wasn't going to tell Da.

Da would never find out.

She'd even begun thinking of round two...when a knock came at the door.

Chapter Nine

Shivawn froze at the sound. Connor's body beside hers was solid, reassuring, but his heartbeat under her ear had jumped.

Who's at my door at this time of night?

Silence.

She lay, tense, against him, and considered easing out of bed to find out who was there.

Don't want to.

A breath of air opened between them. He was ahead of her, silently sliding out from beside her.

A second knock came. A rap-rap-rap, distinctly angry.

"Wait," she whispered, her voice hoarse with sudden terror. "It's *Da*."

Connor stopped, shoulders tense. Back to her, he rasped out, "You don't want him to find me here?"

"He *can't*, Connor." She remembered how, in his fury, he'd hurt Uncle Seamus. "You have no idea how he gets, what he'll say, what he'll *do*—"

"Will he hurt you?" He spun on that, chest heaving, pectorals and biceps tense to the point she could see the striations. The barely leashed fury and determination on his face said exactly what he'd do to any man who abused her.

"No! No, of course not." Hastening to reassure him, she scooted out of bed and began hunting for her clothes. "It's just that he's already on edge because of the competition. I don't want him getting any wrong ideas about us." Bad from a number of standpoints, like the very real possibility he'd toss her out like Uncle Seamus. The obvious impact on their chances in the Battle of the Bands was overshadowed by what it would do to the band, the family. And just at the edge of possibility was the horrific idea that Da might actually be hurt by what he would think of as her disloyalty.

Connor watched her closely. "You don't want our relationship to start out on a bad note?"

A shiver went through her. *Our relationship.*

There wouldn't be one if Connor and Da faced off.

"Go wait in the bathroom. I'll take care of it." Dressed, she pressed past him, stopping at the door when he didn't move.

His whole demeanor shouted his reluctance to leave her, to hide. She glanced out the peephole in case she was wrong and it was a random drunk knocking mistakenly at her door instead of an irate Irish father.

But no. There was Da, his face redder than usual, his gaze hard with suspicion.

Urgency bled through her. She turned a pleading gaze on Connor, who, after a close, hard study of her face, spun and stalked to the bathroom, snatching up his clothes and shoes along the way. He stomped barefoot into the small room, leaving the door open a crack.

With a deep sigh, she pushed on the door handle to release the lock.

Da's slapped hand on the door opened it to the width of the slide. His gaze ran up her fully clothed body to nail her in the eye. "Why are you still dressed?"

Too late she realized she should have put on her nightshirt instead of street clothes.

"Um…I just got in?" *Weak, Shivawn.* Mindful of the sexy bassist in her bathroom, she kicked off an aggressive defense instead. "I had to talk Uncle Seamus down. Shame on you, Da. You shouldn't have been so hard on him."

"Bah. It was just a little dressin' down."

"A *little?* You fired him, for goodness sake!"

"He knows I didn't mean it. Let me in, Siobhán."

Her heart gave a little kick. Too bad she couldn't improvise like Connor. Maybe if she thought in chords, she'd have come up with a better comeback than, "I would, b-but…but I'm tired. I'm going to bed now. I don't mean to be rude, but, goodnight, Da—"

"Is Maggie in there with you, then?" His tone was pleasant. Too pleasant.

"Um, no?" She sensed a trap, but not the direction it lay. "She's partying. With one of the bands. One that didn't make it." Close enough to the truth, far enough from S-E-X, where she thought the land mine was. Sure, she and Margaret were both adults, but their parents didn't want to know that.

"Is she? What was that noise, then, earlier?"

"Noise?" She swallowed, hard, because her mouth was suddenly dry. How long had he been standing outside the door?

"When I passed here earlier, to make sure you were in for the night. Getting your rest. But before I could knock, I thought I heard a radio playing."

"A radio?" She tried to improvise. "Oh, that was probably me, doing some last-minute brush-up practicing. I guess I've been here longer than I thought."

"No, not you. I heard a bass thumping through. Jazz, or maybe rhythm & blues. The longer I listened, the more I knew that was no radio." As he spoke, his brow lowered and furrowed until he developed an downright scary scowl. "That was *live*."

He'd heard Connor playing. She tried not to gasp and scrambled for an explanation.

"Open the door, Siobhán. Let me see for myself that no one is here, as you say. Then I'll be sleeping more peacefully tonight."

She clenched the handle on her side. He didn't mean to be this harsh, this controlling. She had to remember he'd missed most of her childhood through no fault of his own. Maybe, like she tried to be obedient to make him happy, he was acting overly strict to make up for not being there when she was a child. It wouldn't hurt to show him quick, to reassure him.

Still, her stomach churned anxiously when, with a quick glance at the cracked bathroom door, she let her father in. He marched past her without words, but his stomping clearly voiced his frustration and anger.

He stopped abruptly. "*That*." He pointed at the guitar, laying on Maggie's bed. "What's that doing here?" His red face, strangely, had gone pale.

"Oh, um, well, Margaret met a nice musician from one of the country bands. They, um, dropped off their instruments before going to party. He might have played a little for her before they went."

"A country band, hmm?" His color returned as he eyed her. "That's like an American céilí band, I'm supposing? Not so bad. At least they follow tradition."

"Yes," Shivawn agreed quickly, relieved. "And they're definitely not one of our competitors. She wouldn't betray the family like that." She winced, hearing it from her own mouth. Maggie wasn't, but *she* was.

Connor isn't the enemy, she argued with herself. *Da is just being uptight.*

"It's not that, Siobhán." His gaze came back to her, frustration of a different sort crowding out the anger. "Or not *just* that. I'm trying to keep you both safe."

"Safe?" *From what, out-of-tune notes?* "They're all musicians, Da. Like us."

"Not all of them," he ground out. "The rock-and-roll hooligans—they're seductive. Not making good, clean dancing music but bumping and grinding and singing about sex and drugs."

"They're *musicians*," she repeated, bewildered. "Even if their music isn't quite like ours—"

"They're beguiling bastards, I tell you." He underscored his frustration with a slash of hand. His gaze kept flicking back to the electric bass. "You're a good girl, telling me the truth, aren't you, Siobhán? You wouldn't fib about where that thing came from?"

Her stomach dropped into her feet. *He knows.*

No, he didn't. He couldn't. *And anyway, it's none of his business.*

Then why did she feel so guilty?

"I told you." She nervously fingered the notch at her neck. "It belongs to Maggie's boy."

Pain shuttered his gaze. He didn't believe her.

Her heart iced with guilt. *Why should he believe me? I'm lying. I've done what Da asked me not to do. I'm lying and I'm hiding Connor from him.*

The urge to come clean surged up inside her like lava up a volcano. *Tell Da about Connor.*

But that was madness. Da would blow up. She didn't want to deal with his anger, and more, she didn't want to cause him further pain.

He might see my taking up with a rival as big a betrayal as Mom's leaving.

Caught on the swords of her own best intentions, she tried, "Da, I don't understand. Why are you getting so worked up over a boy's guitar?"

"An *electric* guitar." The words exploded from him.

"But what's wrong with that? He's just another musician—"

"That's what *she* said." His fists balled, his cheeks purpled, and his breath chugged like a locomotive.

Alarm for him warred with her confusion. *She?*

"She said he was safe. She said he loved her. But he didn't, and he took her from us."

"Her, who, Da? *Who—*?"

"Annie. He took our Annie!" He stood rigid, all his muscles tight and trembling, his chest pummeling as if it was the only release for his emotion.

Bewildered, scared, she barely managed to connect the name. Da's sister? The one she'd never met. *"A great tragedy."* Shivawn always assumed disease had claimed her. She ventured, "Aunt Annie died young."

"She died because a *boy* lured her away." Da whirled to jab a finger at Connor's bass. "He introduced her to new music. Rock and roll. He also introduced her to sex—and drugs."

She'd never heard this before. Her cheeks went cold and any reply dried up in her throat.

"'Twas the bloody drugs which took her life."

"D-drugs?" Her throat thickened. She tottered on trembling legs to the corner chair and collapsed on the large footstool. "Aunt Annie died from drugs?"

"A great tragedy."

She'd never even considered this.

"The feckin' poison was the weapon, but that boy killed her." He stomped to where Shivawn sat, put his face right by hers. "The bloody stuff wouldn't have gotten its claws in her, if not for him," he spat.

His breath blew across her face, hot as an angry storm. She trembled in its ferocity.

"We knew something was wrong but not what. Annie started coming to céilí band practice later and later. And then she started skipping." He straightened, gaze over her head. "I tried to tell Mam, but..." His voice cracked. "I was too young. 'Let her sow her wild oats,' Mam said. So I left it alone." He fell silent, jaw clenching.

Shivawn waited, hunched on the ottoman, stomach churning an iceberg of anxiety. The real reason Da insisted on punctuality for practice was more terrible than she could have imagined. She dreaded to hear the rest of the story.

"Sometimes Annie would come to band and be her old self. But sometimes..." His tone thickened and he turned away, swallowing hard. "Sometimes she played with a fever that consumed her. She got thinner and thinner. More and more manic."

"The drugs?" Shivawn croaked.

He made a deep, unhappy noise. His gaze was glued to Connor's guitar. "Before that boy"— he spat the word—

"Annie got high on playing. But after, music wasn't enough. She was always after a newer, better high. The music...it wasn't enough at the end. Only the drugs." His voice broke, and he looked away.

"I'm sorry," she whispered, her heart breaking for him. She understood her father better, his strictness an armor from having lost a beloved sister so harshly when he was so young.

His gaze came back to her, eyes shimmering with unshed tears. "Annie sold the fiddle, Siobhán. Sold my mam's fiddle."

Shock sent her reeling straight. Her hand pressed to her chest as if she could hold back the new heartache. She knew how much that fiddle meant to him. *When you play it right, Mam's smile will light Heaven itself.*

He dug savagely at his eyes with forefinger and thumb. "She sold Mam's fiddle for money to buy more feckin' drugs."

Not knowing what to say, Shivawn stood and slid her hands onto his shoulders, intending a comforting hug. His muscles were as tense as strings about to snap, startling her into releasing him and blurting, "I-I'm truly sorry, Da."

"*Sorry?*" he snarled. He spun away, stalked off a pace, then snapped around to glare at her, his blue eyes blazing. "That's what *she* said, after she sold my mam's own fiddle! But *sorry* didn't bring that fiddle back. Only a shite-ton of hard work got enough money for that. Not yet sixteen, and I worked my fingers to the bone to get it out of hock." He stomped back to stab a stiff finger into her breastbone. "For *you.*"

If he'd stabbed her with a knife, it couldn't have cut deeper. A jagged lump of cold sat heavy in her chest. "I didn't know."

His chest pumped like a bellows. "She bought drugs with that money—'twas the hit that killed her." Abruptly, he stopped breathing, his lids clenched tight. A single tear slid out from under. "Mam..." He gulped air. "She died from the shock." His eyes snapped open, blazing with hate at the guitar on the bed. "And none of it would have happened if Annie hadn't been seduced by that feckin' boy and his rock and roll."

Shivawn's heart stuttered with pain for him—and herself. Her gaze shifted to the bed where she'd found such happiness. She wanted to come clean about Connor but now knew the cost for Da would be pure anguish.

"So now, Siobhán."

His tone, a low growl, snapped her eyes to him. The blue fury of his gaze hit her with a shock that made her belly quiver.

"I'm asking you one last time. Where did *that* come from?" Venom filled his gaze as he struck a hard finger at the bass guitar.

Stomach roiling, she tried one last time to spare him. "I-I told you. Maggie's friend dropped it off here—"

"Siobhán Ó Dubhda Kelly, you're *lying!*" He grabbed her by the wrist and dragged her off the ottoman. Dropping into the chair, he snarled. "You will tell me the truth, for your own good, or I'll turn you over my knee."

A yank on her wrist told her he was actually serious. "Da, don't."

"I'll spank you so hard you'll not sit down for a week—"

"You won't lay a hand on her," Connor ripped out, launching himself from the bathroom. "If you try, you do it through *me*."

A rush of primitive elation filled Shivawn's chest at his dashing to the rescue, almost immediately trounced by the reality of how this looked. "Connor," she groaned.

Thankfully fully dressed, he wedge himself between her and Da, forcing him to let her go. Then he stood beside her, fists clenched, his body flared big and rigid and ready to defend her.

His chivalry both touched and unnerved her. If he'd heard Da's story at all, he knew the situation was volatile like a roomful of gas vapor.

Da was silent, but only for a moment. Then he jumped to his feet with a roared, "Who the hell are *you?*"

"Da, this is Connor." This would be bad. Shivawn stepped out from behind her knight's bulwark body, swallowing a thousand thick regrets. If only she'd openly defied her father's demands from the start. If she'd been up front with him, it wouldn't have come to this. But how could she have known she'd mesh with Connor so quickly, so perfectly? This would be terrible, the maelstrom in her chest told her, and there was no way to make it better. "He's with Taboo Soul."

Her father's jaw clenched as if he was grinding his molars. "He's with that *rock* band."

"He's someone I l-like, Da. Someone I wanted to g-get to know better." *Damn it, not now.* She needed to speak clearly. Calmly. She took a deep breath and pushed out her fears and frustrations on a puff of air. "Let's talk this over like adults—"

"I told you. It's how we lost Annie!" He pointed an accusing finger at Connor...which trembled and fell. "How we lost...I lost poor A-Annie." Abruptly, he shoved past them both, stopping just short of the bed with its damning guitar, his shoulders heaving with a throttled sob. "Now I've lost you," he whispered.

She'd been so sure of herself. So sure she was doing the right thing, inviting Connor up. That she could keep it from impacting her father.

As Da shuffled to the door and shambled out of the room, a broken man, Shivawn's heart shattered.

She pressed back a sob, covering her mouth with both hands. *What have I done?*

*　　*　　*

Connor's insides twisted as Shivawn turned from him. Her eyes were cast down, but he'd caught the glitter of tears beneath her lashes.

"Maybe you'd better go."

He'd known what she was going to say. After hearing her father's confession, he understood why she said it. But he didn't regret a moment of what had passed between them. He'd felt the link from the first time he saw her, the first time he heard her music.

What he and she had done together in this bedroom only made him more sure of their connection. Though he knew why, and his heart hurt for her, he said, "I think my leaving is a mistake. But if that's what you want…"

He waited a moment, not because he expected her to change her mind, but because he hoped. But no signal came.

Connor nerved himself to walk away. As he passed, her gaze rose and met his. Her beautiful eyes were sad. Resigned.

Troubled.

Damn it. He'd honor her words and leave—*after this.*

Hoping like hell he was doing the right thing, he wrapped her in his arms, ready to let her go instantly if she said or did anything that gave the slightest indication his embrace was unwelcome.

She pressed her head into his chest with an aborted sob.

Arms tightening around her, he murmured soothing words and held her as she trembled against him. He began stroking her head. She made no sound, but his shirt front dampened.

"Don't regret it," he said impulsively. "What we did together—it was good. You're not your aunt."

"I know." She pulled away, sniffing and rubbing her eyes. "Connor, I-I really loved what we did...together. But..." Her gaze shifted to the side. "But for now, it's better if we don't see each other. Don't talk."

"It's *not* better." His words forced themselves past a constricted throat.

She heaved a watery breath and finally looked at him. "Maybe not for you and me. But it's better for Da, and right now, I have to think of him. Look, our band tours all summer, but come fall I teach school and Da goes back to Ireland. Maybe after that we can..." She trailed off, searching his eyes.

He understood what she needed from him, knew she wanted him to say, *"Yes, your father comes first. Yes, I'll wait."* He understood he was new. Her father had been part of her entire life—she loved her da, but she didn't yet know if she loved Connor.

Although he was pretty sure he was falling in love with her.

He wanted to give her what she needed. But inside, he couldn't get past the fact she was choosing a man who yelled at her, who grabbed her wrist and threatened to hit her, over him.

That bitterness bled through into his gaze: he knew it the instant her cheeks darkened and she looked away with a sigh.

Something inside him withered at the sound.

"Or maybe not," she finally said. "But in any case, this is what I need to do right now."

He opened his mouth to say, *"I understand."* He tried. But his heart didn't understand. It was weeping.

Silently, he secured the guitar in its case then unplugged his amp and slowly wrapped the cords. His joints ached as if he'd aged twenty years.

Tucking the amp under one arm, he slid his guitar case off the spare bed and turned.

She looked anywhere but at him. No tears remained in her eyes, but that was all right. His heart cried enough for both of them.

Chapter Ten

Shivawn forced herself not to reach out as Connor passed her without a word and let himself out. She made herself undress and go to bed, but she tossed and turned the rest of the night. She'd disappointed Da and alienated Connor.

She didn't like disappointing people in general, but disappointing people she loved made her ache inside. Strangely, she ached as much about Connor as Da.

So she was awake and cranky by the time her alarm went off for the Kelly band eight a.m. rehearsal.

Da had reserved the room optimistically labeled Grande Gallery. It was more the size of a cramped den, but if they all sucked in their breath, they fit.

Everyone was there but for Da. Uncle Seamus stood in the corner, a hangdog expression on his face. Not gone yet, but on the fringes, his tenure dependent on Da's mood.

Which, after last night's debacle in her room, wouldn't be good. She hadn't done Uncle Seamus any favors by hooking up with Connor last night.

To her surprise and relief, Da came breezing in, scowling to be sure, but only his normal scowl. "We won our bracket," he announced sternly, "But *barely*. Seamus, what the feck are you doing hunched over there? 'Drowsy Maggie' from the top."

They all scrambled to obey. Shivawn, in between doing her damnedest to remember the new ornamentations, tried to catch her father's eye.

As they swung around to the top, he cut her an annoyed glance.

She shot him a hopeful smile. *Are we okay?*

He rolled his eyes and snorted. She could practically hear his, *Are ye daft? Of course we're okay. We're family.*

Relief flooded her, which of course was when she reverted to the old ornaments.

Da cut them off. "No, no! Flute and fiddle, get your feckin' cuts together. Seamus, the balance is all off."

She clamped her lips together. Amplification would take care of that, but, after the firing fiasco and the bedroom disaster, mentioning amps might be the match to Da's temper.

Cousin Liam, who'd missed both, didn't have a clue. "If we'd just amplify the hammered dulcimer and mandolin—"

"*No.*" Da scowled thunderclouds at them all. "We will play this as the Kellys played it before us!"

Before last night, she would have thought he was mired in the last century. Now, she understood this was how he showed his love for his family, his own da and mam. How he fiercely defended that love.

How he covered his heart, aching for his sister, lost to radical ideas and times.

But she also remembered the brilliance and electricity of her music with Connor last night. Amplification wasn't radical anymore. Rock and roll was the norm.

And frankly, she was worried tradition wouldn't win them the judges—or the audience, whose vote was equal in round three.

"All right, from the top." Da circled one finger in the air in a play-it-again motion. "And for feck's sake, let's get it *right* this time. We've got a competition to win!"

His fierce need echoed in her heart. She wanted to win the Battle of the Bands for him, especially now that she knew what he'd suffered to get here, what it meant to him.

But she also started wondering if "right" was going with tradition—or against it.

*   *   *

Sleeping badly, Connor rose early. He sleep-walked his way past a snoring Zach and their light guy Dan on his cot, gradually woke up in the shower, and cleared out of the room as everyone else stirred. Making his way to the hotel lobby, he found a chair sheltered by ferns and sat. The band was meeting for breakfast to discuss their final rehearsal for tonight, and he was a full half-hour early, but he needed the quiet time alone to think.

He mulled over Shivawn's decision to distance herself. Though he knew why she'd made that decision—he couldn't forget the pain in her eyes at her father's broken admission—and he certainly respected her wishes and would stay away, his own wishes were fervently different.

Making love with Shivawn had been more than sex, it was connecting, heart to heart.

"That kay-lee band is a problem."

Connor's ears pricked. Who was talking about Shivawn's group?

107

"Them, and that Taboo Soul. We don't have to worry about that beach band or The Harmonizers."

He peered through the fronds of the palm and recognized the man he'd put to bed last night, Townshend, talking to the drummer of The Battre, plus a petite, bearded guy Connor didn't recognize. They were talking about their competitors, like every other band here.

It didn't reassure him.

"So, who are the key musicians in the Kelly group?" the bearded man asked.

Connor frowned. Bands likely to place ahead of them, okay—that was just scoping out the competition. But key members? Worry gnawed at his gut.

"Their leader is the old man. That Paddy Kelly. His sister's a dragon, so she's probably a force, too. But the real danger is that fiddle player."

Shivawn. He didn't like them talking about her at all.

"She didn't do so good last night," the other band member said.

"Aw, Platt was just blowing smoke. He doesn't like freaky gifted showoffs any more than I do. Anyway, she might have just been off her game last night—you should've seen her during the open playoffs. She took over the stage like she owned it. If she'd had proper lighting and a solo spot, she would've had the whole room eating from the palm of her hand."

Townshend spoke with strangely vying amounts of admiration, sick fascination, and loathing in his tone.

A shiver of dark foreboding shook Connor to his core.

"So, what's the plan?" the drummer asked.

"Well..."

He sat with every muscle tensed, listening hard. A ding percussed the air, the elevator arriving. As another band emptied out, laughing and talking, Townshend shut up. He and his cronies filed outside with the band.

Leaving Connor churning with sick dread.

*   *   *

That evening, Shivawn and her family sat in a line along the Starstruck main bar and listened to the last five brackets play. She was surprised to see all five bands who'd won last night arrayed at the bars. But then, on reflection, they were here for the same reason her family were—to get a feel for the competition.

Da found them six places together. They sat facing out to watch the bands, Cousin Margaret with her elbows against the rail beside Shivawn.

Ultra-sexy bartender Ben, who she'd found out was Rusty's son, immediately slid up behind Maggie. "Margarita? Or something different tonight?" He tinted "something different" with just enough sexual innuendo be enticing without lopping over into *seriously?*

To her surprise, Maggie simply looked over her shoulder and shrugged. "Surprise me."

Ben's expression turned shrewd, and his gaze laser-pointed along where hers had been a moment before. He must've seen something because his practiced smile morphed into a real grin. "Darlin', you've just surprised me, and that's not easy to do. This one's on the house." He dipped a glass in salt, a perfect circular rim. Pulling a pitcher from below, he poured her a margarita on the rocks.

Curious, Shivawn tried to see where Maggie had been looking, too. There was Taboo Soul, in a bunch like the Kellys. Her gaze homed in instantly on Connor, her heart beating momentarily harder. Forget absence making the heart grow fonder, now that she knew what his muscles felt like under that T-shirt of his—and how perfectly both their bodies and their hearts meshed—she only wanted him more.

Maybe feeling her gaze burning on him, his switched toward her. Their eyes met for an instant. Cutting a quick glance at Da to make sure he wasn't looking, Connor dipped an acknowledging nod at her. No more. No band members were cross-fraternizing tonight.

Except for one.

As Ben the bartender slid a beer the color of amber crystal at her elbow, the small guy with the bowl haircut and skinny suit sidled up on her other side—the one from The Battre Beatles tribute band who'd looked at them so strangely that first morning.

"Hi." He yelled it over the current band, a heavy metal group with all their knobs set to twenty.

"Hi." She kept her gaze on the band.

"I don't think we've been properly introduced. I'm Roger Townshend."

"Shivawn." She thought about adding, *What can I do for you*, for politeness sake, but something about him made her squeamish about prolonging the conversation.

Didn't stop him. "We're giving a party tonight. I'm here to invite your band."

"We're already invited to a party." Which was true. Rusty had reserved a room upstairs for all the winners. Shivawn was planning to go. There'd be cake.

"An after-party party. All the winning bands will be there."

Even Taboo Soul? Her heart rate picked up. She didn't want to rile Da, but if there was even a chance of seeing Connor, a chance to be in the same room with him...

"See you there, then." He went to Da next. Her father wasn't listening, but Aunt Katie was, so she knew they'd go.

"Look out for him." Ben had been in the background, wiping a glass, but now he stepped forward, a narrowed gaze on Townshend. "I don't like him."

She frowned at him over her shoulder. "Why?"

"Bartender!" A lady down the way waved a twenty.

He just shook his head at Shivawn and went to serve the woman.

Unease rumpled her nape. But if Connor would be there, it might be worth going. She'd just have to be careful.

Chapter Eleven

Across the Starstruck dance floor, Connor noted the Battre guy stop beside where Shivawn stretched her beautiful body out on a barstool. His stomach filled with acid. He didn't know what Townshend was saying, but her expression turned contemplative, as if she was considering his words.

He didn't trust anything coming out of that snake's mouth.

His feet itched to go to her. He knew she'd rather not risk Paddy Kelly seeing them together, but he needed to find out what crap Townshend was peddling. After hearing the guitarist talking about her just this morning, he would rather risk Kelly's feelings than Shivawn's safety.

Decision made, he rose from his barstool.

Daw, their lead singer, grabbed him by the biceps. "Whatcha doing, man?"

Connor shook off his grip, gaze locked on Shivawn. Where, with a smile, Townshend nodded and moved jauntily toward the rest of her family.

"None of your business."

"Except, it looks like you're headed over to chat up one of those luscious Kellys. It's my business if you're hanging with the enemy."

Connor's gaze snapped to Daw.

"Yeah." Behind Daw, Hanson, the lead guitarist, glowered. "It's *all* our business. 'Specially after last time."

Connor closed his lids against an eyeroll.

"Truth, now." The singer's tone was deliberately provocative. "You looking for some hot Kelly action?"

The crude innuendo annoyed him, and he snapped his eyes open. "If you must know, I saw the guy from The Battre talking with the Kelly band. I don't trust him. I want to warn her—them."

His band mates exchanged a significant glance. "Hell, man," Daw said. "Then it's exactly like last time."

Damn it. They still thought he was a paranoid boob. One mistaken attempt at helping six months ago, but he'd be paying for it for years. "Look, the only thing I want to know is what Townshend said. He talked to you, too, Daw. What did he want?"

The singer put a placating hand on his shoulder. "Settle, buddy. Don't make a fool of yourself." The *again* was implied.

He raised a challenging brow. "Tell me what he wanted, and I'll let it go."

"If you're really ready to let it go," Daw countered, "then just trust me."

Trust him? With Shivawn's safety on the line? *Not a chance in hell.*

He tore himself away from the singer's grip.

It wasn't paranoia, it was being prepared.

He hadn't gotten two steps toward her when his friend and band mate, Zach, intercepted him, grabbing one shoulder. His expression was desperate.

"Connor, bud, I need your help."

Gaze locked on Shivawn, Connor resisted the urge to pop his friend's hold with a punishing fist. "In a minute. I have something to do first—"

"I don't have a minute. I might only have one chance at this, and I need you now."

Zach's urgency grated against Connor's, sparking embers of irritation in his blood. He cut a glance at his friend. "What?"

"That pretty little redhead might give me a dance—but you have to distract her dragon of a mother."

Redhead? Was Zach after Shivawn? Embers lit into a bonfire...

Dragon echoed a memory, and his anger banked. "Who?"

"I'd point, but I don't want to alert the dragon. Margaret Clancy. *Maggie.*" Zach sighed the name like a simpering idiot.

Connor would've rolled his eyes, but he supposed he had it as bad for Shivawn.

"I saw her the first night we were here, but she was pretty tight with that country singer. They argued this morning, though, so I went over to talk with her and..." He sighed dreamily again. "I'd just go ask her to dance, but apparently her mother has a problem with rock musicians."

Poor Zach. It decided him. "Yes, all right. I'll help you. Let's go." And right after, he'd warn Shivawn.

They crossed the floor together, cutting like a ship's prow through the dancers moving to the current band, a hip-hop group called Unforgettable Life. The group was energetic and charismatic, with a good beat and scintillating rhythm going. Connor grimaced. They'd not only win their bracket, but their keyboard and drummer would probably get added to Townshend's key players list.

The nearer he got to Shivawn, the harder it was not to look at her. As he and Zach approached the main bar, Connor forced himself to focus on Margaret Clancy.

Margaret's gaze flicked toward Zach. No recognition or encouragement gleamed in her blue eyes. He was almost disappointed in her—his friend was a great guy. Then he caught her cheeks pinking as she adjusted her position on the barstool, from sprawled against the rail to curled appealingly.

He smiled to himself. *So Zach's right. She is interested.*

As his buddy peeled off toward Margaret Clancy, Connor's feet took him automatically toward Shivawn. Paddy Kelly had gone off to the restrooms, but duty first. Connor forced himself to bypass Shivawn and headed for Margaret's mother, Katie Clancy.

As he approached, he made sure to catch Katie's attention with a smile. The "dragon" appellation was misleading. She was a beautiful older woman. Only the hard blue glint of her eye following him as he approached and the slight brackets beside her mouth hinted at her inner strength.

The glint turned to suspicion when he stopped before her, hands in his pockets. Not paranoia—the fact was, none of the bands were mixing. He had no reason to be there, smiling at her, except one.

The enemy of my enemy is my friend.

He jacked his chin at Townshend. "What did that dipshit want?"

Her eyes narrowed. "Why do you care?"

"Because he talked to you and to our lead singer. He *didn't* talk to me, and I don't trust him."

At his periphery, he caught Zach leading Maggie Clancy onto the dance floor. He suddenly wished he could dance openly with Shivawn.

"Our singer's an ass," he continued, "and couldn't find food at a grocery store. But you look to be nobody's fool. So I thought I'd ask you."

Katie's mouth twitched, an almost-smile. "Fair enough. The boy invited us to an after-party. *The* after-party, to hear him tell it." She gave a contemptuous snort.

"Then you're not going?"

"On the contrary. Why not go? It might be amusing. And perhaps our competition will drink too much. Perhaps I can even help." Her smile broadened, teeth bared and almost ripsaw sharp.

"Ah." He glanced down the bar and saw Maggie and Zach shimmying their way into the throng. Friendship duty done, he could now turn his attention to his own goal. "Thanks."

With the pair safely tucked among the crowd, Connor nodded to Katie Clancy and turned toward Shivawn.

But now he had a problem. A *party?* How could he warn her when Townshend was inviting her to so innocuous a thing as a party? Even if he were completely honest with her and explained the nasty vibe he got from The Battre guy, she had no cause to believe him. He'd look like a neurotic jackass.

He sighed. He had to try anyway, because he was worried about her.

Connor focused his gaze on her. She was staring at where Zach and Maggie were barely visible among the dancing throng. Her expression was acute surprise—tinged with a longing that resonated in his gut. Was she wishing *they* could openly dance as much as he?

He stopped, experiencing that profound connection, one he was loathe to break.

But that stop saved him as he caught her father cutting through the dancers from the restrooms, glaring at Connor.

Damn it. He couldn't speak to her now, not even an unexplained glance.

Maybe it was for the best. What did he really have to warn her about? A party pretty much everyone was going to? He was still afraid of coming off like a neurotic jackass.

Later. He'd have to watch carefully for his opportunity.

The last bracket played and was decided. The house band took the stage, and the bars emptied as the bracket competitors, both winners and losers, took the spiral stairs up to the Star Deck. Connor waited until Shivawn headed up, her father tight behind, then wandered upstairs, too.

He kept his gaze on her without being obvious about it. The whole time she was at the party, her father stayed by her side like a goalie defending against a hard press. Every time he looked, there was her da, glaring at him. Connor began to actively dislike pugnacious noses and stormy, gray-blue eyes.

The party broke up around two in the morning, the ten winning bands needing to get back to rest up for the finals, while the losing bands wanted to drown their sorrows with something stronger than champagne punch and cake.

Shivawn headed down the stairs. Her father clumped in her wake, darting periodic glares up at Connor. Pretending disinterest, he stayed where he, but he chafed inside. The moment the pair hit the floor, he joined the throng spiraling down.

But his circumspection worked against him. Shivawn and her father had retrieved their stored instruments and were on their way out before he even got off the stairs. He muscled his way through the still-thick throng, snatched his bass from the back, and shoved with increasing desperation to the door. As she boarded the first waiting bus, Connor dashed into line. But the bus filled up, closed its doors, and took off while he was still halfway back. He raced for the next bus, but it, too, was full.

On the third, he sat staring out the window, case between his knees, twitching as he fought a rising plume of hot irritation meeting the cold pit of worry in his stomach. The buses, chartered specifically for the event, weren't on any set schedule. They ran between the Kramer Hotel in the heart of downtown and Starstruck and took off for the other when filled. So, when the bus was finally full, the engine revved, and they started off, it'd felt like hours to Connor, though it was actually only fifteen minutes later.

Still, it was enough of a delay that, when he raced into the hotel, there was no sign of Shivawn, her father, or any of her family. Acid flooded his stomach as he scanned for them.

"Did you hear about some after-party?" A guy passing him was speaking to the rhythm guitarist for The Beachies.

"Yeah, but it's only for the *stars*," the guitar player sneered. "Not the merely good players, like us."

Key players.

His heart rate spiked. *Fuck it.* Connor had to warn Shivawn. Even if it risked her thinking him a disturbed, overly suspicious ass, he had to act. Hell, he'd even risk going through that pugnacious father of hers.

But how, when he didn't know where she was?

He paced in the lobby, gut churning.

An idea hit him, and he stopped with a snap of his fingers. If she was at Townshend's after-party, maybe it was in Townshend's room. And he knew where that was.

Not even bothering to put his axe in his room, Connor dashed up three flights of stairs.

Four-oh-two was silent. Still, he knocked. No answer.

Fear splashed cold in his veins. He kicked into pacing again, cudgeling his brain for an idea on how to find Shivawn, then lit on calling Zach, who'd probably hooked up with Maggie.

His friend answered with a whispered, "Not now."

"Emergency," he replied shortly. "Are you at the after-party?"

"You might say that." The music in his buddy's tone said it was a party for two.

"Right." Connor hung up. *Damn it.* Now how would he find Shivawn? His mind darkened with anxiety for her.

Think, think. Instead of pacing, he forced himself to lean back against the nearby wall, where he closed his eyes and pictured her. Her vigorous bowing as they played the reel. Her hair shimmering through his fingers. Her face like an angel as she came...

The diner. That morning Rusty had thrown the bands together. Out of general bonhomie? Or had she seen the spark between him and Shivawn and gone out of her way to fan it?

Hoping against hope, he found the number for Starstruck and called. It took him two people and several countless moments on hold, but an hour or minute later, the country music star answered.

"Hey, Connor. Took you long enough," Rusty drawled.

"I, uh..." He was momentarily thrown. She'd *expected* him to call? *No time. Ask.* "Look, I was wondering if you knew—"

"Where Townshend's after-party is? Rumors are the little shit signed out a meeting room for the whole night. Keep that *little shit* comment between us, by the way. As official sponsor of the Battle of the Bands, I have no favorites."

"Thanks, Rusty." He was already headed for the stairwell.

"My pleasure." She hung up.

When he got to the business wing, one of the meeting-room doors was propped open, a sickly sweet odor wafting out like a giggle-smoke snake.

He dropped his case in the hallway and shoved his way in. Yes, he hadn't been invited, but he wasn't going to let that stop him.

The place was packed with drinking, dancing, eating, talking—rather, shouting—people. Music beat the walls, and colored lights pulsed with it like a demented lava lamp. Connor recognized three of the people on Townshend's hit list, Paddy Kelly, Katie Clancy, and Connor's own lead singer Daw, along with several of the winning bands' top musicians. His gut screamed this seemingly innocent party was a trap, but he still didn't understand how.

How didn't matter. Only who. *Key players. Stars.*

All but the one who meant the most to him. The one Townshend had been fixated on.

Shivawn.

Was he too late? Had the snake already done something to her?

Chapter Twelve

"Connor?"

Shivawn's voice floated into his ear from nowhere and everywhere. It seemed like a miracle, that his thoughts of her, his *need* for her, had conjured her.

Paranoid fool. In reality, she'd come in through the door behind him. He spun.

"There you are," he said as she shouted, "What are you doing here?"

They both yelled simultaneously over the party's roar. He stared at her, and she at him. Then they laughed, together. *In perfect sync.*

"Let's go outside," he said. When she nodded, he put his hands on her shoulders, noting she leaned into him with a delicious sort of shiver when he did. That shiver whispered ideas to him, voluptuous, heady ideas of rumpled sheets smelling of satisfaction. It took every bit of self-possession he had to simply steer her out of the room.

The air was quieter and cooler out in the hall.

She nodded at the door. "Da was in there. Do you think he saw me?"

"No. I was blocking the door, and I'm taller than you."

"And broader." She eyed his shoulders, her gaze darkening.

He squared them a bit, unduly pleased.

"What are you doing here?" she asked again. "Are you here for the party?"

He was so relieved to find her all right that he answered without thinking. "No, I had to see you. Make sure you were okay."

"Why wouldn't I be? Connor, is something wrong?"

His stomach dropped. He hadn't thought beyond finding her, getting her out of Townshend's sphere. He'd done that, but how would he keep her out? "Well..." He faltered, not knowing what best to say. He didn't want to lie, not to her, but the truth was so sparse, it'd make him look like a paranoid fool or worse, a control freak. Exposed, vulnerable, he rubbed the back of his neck.

She searched his face. "Something *is* wrong. What's going on? You can tell me. Be honest with me, Connor."

Be honest. Those two words stopped his rubbing. Twin memories reverberated inside him, so hard and bright it robbed him of breath. Opposite sides of the same traumatic coin.

Two people had asked him for the truth. One, he'd told the truth, and Daw taught him honesty only brought him mistrust and broken friendships.

But his young sister...he'd told her a comforting lie that haunted him to this day.

"Connor, look at me." Shivawn palmed his cheeks. "You can tell me." Her expression was earnest, open. She trusted him.

Regret painted another trusting face over hers, the determined, scared eight-year-old that was his sister.

"Am I dying? Be honest with me, Connor."

"No way, squirt. You'll outlive me."

He clenched his eyes against both earnest, beloved faces. A tear squeezed out and trickled down his cheek.

"What's wrong?" Shivawn whispered. "You can tell me."

He'd held his sister's hand one last time, when she finally knew the truth. Her eyes were agonized, but not all of it was the cancer. The worst, the one that cut him deepest, was her pain at his betrayal.

"You could have told me."

No. No, I couldn't.

His sister had died, leaving him alone, only his guilt and misery as company. Daw's abandoning him was a nightmarish echo.

He couldn't take that again.

Shivawn's voice broke into his misery. "You won't tell me?"

"I c-can't." His words were cold, ragged lumps in his throat.

"All right." Her hands dropped from his face.

She's leaving, too. Agony punched a hole in him. His eyes sprang open.

But she'd only removed her hands to wrap her arms around his waist in a tight hug. "Then I'll guess. You don't trust Townshend, but you don't want to tell me why, because it's just a guess—and because someone in your past made you doubt yourself."

"How...?" He gazed down at her in wonder. "You can't know that. You just met me."

"I don't know you—but I know your *music*. And that means I know your *heart*. You're strong and steady and you fight for what's right. And you're passionate. Whatever you did in the past, you did out of love."

A sob rose in his chest. "I'm not sure." His voice came out hoarse. "I lied to someone who mattered. I thought I was doing it to be kind, but maybe I was just afraid. And when I told a friend the truth about his girlfriend... maybe it was because I didn't like her and wanted to make trouble."

"A friend? And this friend didn't already know or guess how you felt? That you weren't exploding inside every time you saw your friend and his girl together? Connor, sometimes you have to say something just to make the best of a bad situation. How the other person deals with it is their choice. Sweetheart—when you finally tell me what you're afraid of, when you honor me by telling me your truth—how I deal with that is *my* choice."

At her words, her earnest shining face, his heart shattered—and was remade.

Haltingly, half-afraid she'd change her tune and leave, he told her exactly what Townshend said. "I don't know what he's planning, or even *if* he's planning something. All I know is I don't trust him."

She put a palm on his chest over his heart, and smiled up at him. "Thank you for telling me."

He searched her face for a clue that she was disappointed in him, but her words rang with conviction, and her face shone just as brightly.

Still, heart in his throat, he had to ask, "So I've told you. Now what will you do? What is your choice?" *Will you leave me like my sister did? Will you push me away like my friend?*

"You'd better go," she said, confirming his worst fears.

"I-if you think it's best." He managed a small smile but couldn't keep the dark unhappiness from his voice.

A puzzled frown crinkled her face as she searched his gaze, almost immediately clearing. "Oh, no. I'm going to try to convince Da to leave the party. He's here to scope out the competition, so it's going to be hard—seeing you would just make it harder."

"Oh." He felt silly and overjoyed and relieved. "Good luck." He bent to give her a quick peck on the cheek.

"I'll need it." She grabbed his ears and brought his face down for a full, lingering kiss.

When she released him a moment later, he was panting, his ears rang, his heart pounded, and he was actually dizzy. The woman could kiss.

"That was for luck?" he managed.

"No. That was for courage." She skimmed past him and into the room.

Smiling, Connor took his case and strode to the end of the hallway, where he waited. If she didn't come out in ten minutes, he was going in after her.

Toe tapping with nerves, he checked his phone time every few seconds. Five minutes went past.

How long does it take to convince one stubborn old man?

He'd just changed his mind and decided to rush in when she emerged, her aunt and father in her wake.

He ducked around the corner, relief spurting in his veins. She was fine.

Now all he had to do was keep his eyes open for any more of Townshend's tricks.

*   *   *

Shivawn woke to a bright and clear morning. *Today's the day.*

Thanks to Connor, whatever awful plan Townshend had in mind for that after-party, she'd gotten Da and Auntie out of danger. Well, if there had been any danger, but she rather thought Connor was right—she'd been getting weird vibes off of Townshend, too. Poor Connor, not able to trust his own instincts.

She jumped out of bed, ready. Excited.

Today we take the stage in the finals. Maybe win us a recording *contract.*

Although, even if the band placed tenth, they still won a fabulous gig. Really, once they got on that stage, there was no way to lose.

Her phone alarm chimed, and she startled. After practice yesterday morning, Da had reserved a conference room for today at nine. When it came to the band, early was on time and on time was late, so she showered, brushed, dressed, and showed up to practice with fiddle in hand at twenty minutes to nine.

Only Uncle Seamus and Cousin Liam were there, one looking dour and the other wholly absorbed in his mandolin.

Cousin Margaret wandered in a few minutes past nine, hair disheveled and wearing her clothes from last night, minus a sock and plus a big grin. Uncle didn't seem to notice.

Odd, she thought. *Da is usually the first one here.* And why was Seamus here without his wife?

"Where's Auntie?" Shivawn asked Uncle Seamus. "And Da?" Their rooms were side by side and connecting, though she hoped for Uncle Seamus's sake the connecting door locked from either side.

"Your aunt was in the shower, slow to wake up. She's not feeling well after last night. Your da was having a spot of stomach trouble."

Probably meaning bitchy hangovers.

Wordlessly, they waited ten long minutes, Liam plinking something modern and chromatic on his mandolin.

No Da. No Aunt Katie. Another five.

Finally Da stumbled in, looking, not pale and hung over, but green. Still, he roared in his usual robust voice, "We've wasted enough time. 'Derry Air.'"

Shivawn exchanged a glance with Maggie. That was "Danny Boy." Most songs, Da set the pace on bodhrán, but "Danny Boy" was a ballad, so there was no drum. Aunt Katie usually launched them off. Well, Katie along with Seamus and Liam, but neither of the men could be heard above the accordion.

Seamus, however, simply nodded, and he and Liam played the three pickups into the first beat. She'd never actually heard their part before beyond a tinkle around the accordion.

Now she was transported into a new world.

"Danny Boy", done with accordion, tugged the heartstrings in a brash sort of way, like a rock ballad. But the hammered dulcimer was like crystalline snow falling and the mandolin added a honeyed shivering over it, like a perfect midwinter night. Liam and Uncle's music filled the room with a shimmering, unearthly beauty.

Then Da came in on the tune in his beautiful Irish tenor, and her heart lurched. Tears actually filled her eyes.

"The summer's gone, and all the flowers dying... Bloody hell!" Da's hands went to his belly.

"Da, what's wrong?" Shivawn barked, stomach dropping. The rest stopped playing, concern on their faces.

The damned wild shites." Da grimaced. "Practice the reel. I'll be back." He slammed out.

Cousin Margaret stared after him. "That must've been some party. I'm almost sorry I missed it."

"Some party, yeah." Shivawn blinked at the slowly closing door, concerned. She'd gotten them out before unnaturally bad things happened, but apparently, not in time to avoid the usual bad things from overindulging at a party.

"So, what do we do now?" Cousin Liam asked.

"Wait for Paddy." Uncle Seamus shrugged and started adjusting the dulcimer's tuning, a never-ending battle. Liam was already off in his own world noodling.

While they waited for Da to come back, Shivawn nudged Maggie with her elbow. "Speaking of missing the party...did I see you with Zach? What happened to Footlong?"

"Oh, I broke up with him."

"You did?" Shivawn smiled. She wondered if her cousin had broken up with Footlong before or after she lost the sock.

Aunt Katie staggered in at that moment. She hadn't even made an attempt at her hair and makeup, utterly un-Katie. Any questions about Maggie's love life dribbled from Shivawn's brain.

"Paddy gave me a message to pass along." She abruptly put a fist to her lips and burped around it. When she got herself under control again, she continued. "Practice is canceled."

"*What?*" Shivawn's disbelief was echoed by several voices.

"He's fountainin', and I'm not much better off." She burped again, going green. "Seamus, run to the drugstore, would you? Get the most heavy-duty medicine you can find."

"Right away, love."

He tucked away his tuner as Aunt Katie, pressing her fist to her lips, ran out. After locking his dulcimer in its case, he hoisted it and followed her. Leaving Shivawn and Maggie staring at each other, stunned.

Into the silence, Liam's plinking dropped loud, followed by his voice. "I wonder if we'll have to forfeit the Battle."

Forfeit? Shock hit her, followed by a flood of disbelief and anger—and a horrific realization.

If another band wanted them out of the way, this might have done it.

Maybe it wasn't simply the usual party over-indulgence. Maybe she hadn't gotten her father and aunt out soon enough after all.

Chapter Thirteen

Shivawn went to her da's room to try to help. Uncle Seamus soon returned with the strongest medicine he could find, and she anxiously awaited improvement. But poor Da and Auntie continued to have a rough time of it.

She tried to get her father to visit urgent care, but the stubborn man kept insisting he'd be fine by that night. She then tentatively broached the idea of forfeiting—to which he replied with a shouted, "Not on your life! That recording contract is ours."

She left him sleeping fitfully and decided to go in search of Connor, to see if any of his band members were similarly afflicted, trying to pin down what had happened. Maybe Townshend had served bad shrimp or something.

The lighting guy let her in. In one corner, Zach bounced sticks on a set of electronic practice pads, a pair of earphones making him deaf to the world. She waved to get his attention.

He removed his earphones. "Sorry. Connor's not here."

Fear gnawing more sharply at her, she thanked him and returned to her room to think where he might be—and found him knocking at her door.

Connor's face was drawn in lines of concern. After a brief greeting kiss, he asked, "Are any of your band sick today?"

She let him into her room. "I was going to ask you the same thing. Yes. Da and Aunt Katie both. You think Townshend did this?" Anger on behalf of Da spiked her blood.

"Not that we can prove." He blew a disgusted breath. "Daw and Hanson are groaning and fighting for the bathroom, but they insist it's only from overindulging. Nobody can prove it's anything but 'some party last night.'"

"Maybe it isn't intentional. Food poisoning?" she said doubtfully. "The symptoms work. Depending on the strain, it takes a few hours to a couple days to show, then anywhere from a day to a couple weeks to finish."

"Except Dan, our light guy, went to the party, and he's okay. Not everyone at the party got sick. Only the 'key' players." He said it with a disgusted face.

She remembered him telling her about Townshend talking with his keyboardist and a bearded guy. "Well, food poisoning or not, the meds Uncle Seamus got better do the trick. Da is still intending to perform tonight."

"The show must go on?" Connor shook his head with a small snort of disbelief. "I guess stubbornness runs in the family."

Mildly insulted, she aimed a scowl at him. "Hey. Watch it."

"Sorry. I meant to say he's stubborn, you're resolute." He smiled. "Forgive me?"

She laughed. "How can I not?" That sexy smile curled warmth into her belly. She had a passing thought as to the next time they might put her empty bed to use when a knock came at the door.

Distracted by thoughts of Connor and bed, she didn't check the peephole before opening the door.

Uncle Seamus eased past her into the room.

Apprehension tightened her muscles and locked her limbs. Da had a fit finding Connor here, before. What would Uncle do?

"I just wanted to let you know I'm going out for stronger medicine...hello, who is this?" His bright eyes had landed on Connor.

She grimaced, not wanting a repeat of night before last but not knowing how to stop it. She braced herself for a scathing rebuke or worse. And Seamus said...

"Oh, you're the bassist from Taboo Soul. Brilliant playing, my lad."

Shivawn's heart thumped in surprise, but Connor only grinned.

"Thanks. Nice hammered dulcimer."

"What you can hear," Seamus scoffed. "Aye, well, I'll just leave you two young people alone." And he let himself out.

"That was surreal," she said.

Connor stared at the door, a bemused smile on his face. "I think we've all been thrown by this illness. Why don't we see if anyone else is reporting sick band members?"

"Or we could stay here for an hour or so." She meant to say it teasingly, but it came out a bit wistful.

"That's more tempting than you know." His gaze flicked to the bed, his expression filled with longing. "But could you guarantee no more Kellys would burst in on us?"

That goosed a laugh from her. "Good point. Let's go see what we can dig up."

They canvassed all the bands, knocking from room to room in their block plus checking with the groups rehearsing in the meeting rooms. Not all the bands were affected—only those standing a chance of winning.

"Suspicious." With each new reported case, Shivawn's anxiety grew.

"Yes. But we can't prove anything." Connor's mouth was grim, his gaze dark.

"Do we have to?" She checked the time. Just enough to clean up and dress for tonight's performance, assuming they were doing one. She headed for the elevator. "Maybe we can just tell Rusty."

"I think Rusty will have already heard." He came with her into the elevator and pushed the button for her floor. "But what can she reasonably expected to do?"

Shivawn mulled that over until they got to her room and inside.

"I'd better let you get ready." Connor kissed her. "Good luck, tonight."

"Thanks. We'll need it." She stretched onto her toes to brush lips against his again. Something about his comforting size and the heat of his breath reassured her. Though she knew time was short, she clung to his mouth a little longer.

Even when she finally released his lips, she found herself reaching for his hand. "I wish you didn't have to go."

"I have to check on Daw and Hanson. But even if our band doesn't play, I'll be there, tonight." He smiled gently. "Nothing will stop me from being with you."

"Thanks." The reassurance lifted a heavy weight from her chest. "Well, I only have half an hour to dress, and I'll have to rush as it is—"

"Hey, Shivawn." The door flew open, Cousin Margaret dashing in. She grabbed a hang-up bag, shoved past, and shut herself into the bathroom.

"Check that." Shivawn sighed. "I only have half an hour to get ready, and now no bathroom."

He laughed. "You look great to me."

A little feather of pleasure tickled her. "Your optometrist is failing you. But I'll take it as a compliment." She laid out her performance outfit then removed her daytime earrings.

"I guess I'll go get ready, too. If there's anything to get ready for." He went to the room's door, stopped, and sighed. "I was looking forward to playing tonight. Not even because of the competition and prizes. I just wanted to play at Starstruck one more time. The crowd will be amazing."

In the middle of fastening a dangle of glittering gold to her lobe, she lifted her gaze to him in the mirror. He looked so sad. Sorrow for him pierced her chest. She'd forgotten, in the midst of all her family's trouble, that he'd lost just as much. Her heart went out to him. She'd do anything to lift some of that sadness.

An idea struck her. "Connor, if your band can't perform—you could play with us. I could ask Da."

He gave a half-hearted laugh. "Stubborn, remember?"

After he'd gone, she chewed it over as she'd finished getting ready. Her father wouldn't like it, with his emphasis on traditional, but for Connor's sake, she'd try. She took her fiddle case up to her father's room, going over alternate arguments the whole way. "We could use a real bass, Da. He won't get to play otherwise. He's too good not to play."

But the moment Da opened the door to her, any arguments died

He was pale and sweaty.

"You're dehydrated." She practically screeched it, but she couldn't help herself. She dropped the fiddle inside the door. "You should go to the hospital!"

"I'm fine. Uncle Seamus's new pills would bind an elephant." He threw a couple small tablets in his mouth, lifting a bottle of red fluid. "Plus a cartload of this electrolyte-balancing stuff." He took a swig and swallowed with a grimace. "Tastes like cherry spit. I'm just about to shower. We'll be taking the stage tonight no matter what."

"No! It's not worth it, Da, not worth you maybe getting sicker—"

"*Bollocks*. I said we're playing, and *we're playing!* Now, get out so I can finish changing. I'll meet you at the bus."

Chafing, she went downstairs to wait. Stubborn? Connor didn't know the half of it.

When her father came downstairs, she tried to get him to reconsider. Da didn't even seem to hear her, strutting past her with his bodhrán, pride and concentration on his face in equal measure, both in stark contrast to his pale skin.

She grimaced. The performance was already on—not for the audience but the psychological one for the other bands. Squaring her shoulders, she followed. But inside, she was crying.

Standing tall and proud, every member of the Kelly Traditional Céilí Band mounted the steps to the bus. The moment Da got in his seat, though, he hunched over as if he had the mother of all cramps. He was up and in line before the bus even pulled to a stop in front of Starstruck, performance forgotten, everything forgotten in his rush down the stairs and out the door, while the rest of them still gathered their cases.

Aunt Katie was better off, but not by much as she minced into the bar and straight back to the ladies' restroom.

Fingers tapped Shivawn's arm. She turned to see Uncle Seamus nodding at the music bag slung over his shoulder. He carefully slid a peek of a bottle of sports drink from his bag. She nodded her understanding—outside food and drink were prohibited. She glanced at Cousin Margaret, but with only her flute case, she had no way to hide it. Seamus surreptitiously passed Shivawn the bottle. Hiding it in her own bag, she nonchalantly traipsed to the ladies' restroom, where she brushed her hair until the main area was empty. A quick glance under the stall doors netted Aunt Katie's black and green patent pumps.

She stuck the bottle under the door. "Auntie." It disappeared with a yank from her hand.

When Shivawn reemerged, Uncle Seamus slid her another bottle. She gave him a puzzled frown. Wasn't Da in the gents?

"I'll wait for your aunt," Seamus said. "You know where our green room is tonight?"

"Back corridor?"

"Yes."

The first four days, all the bands stored cases in a guarded storage room. The bar's green room—a lounge or makeup room set aside for performers—was only for the bands about to go onstage.

But tonight, Rusty had opened the offices upstairs as preparation areas. A pair of bands shared each of four rooms. The Kellys had been assigned the fifth—the actual green room on the main floor. They were sharing it with folk trio John, Jack, and Cherry.

Shivawn entered to see Cherry busy warming up. But both John and Jack were staring at the closed bathroom door in consternation. An uneasy feeling skittered over her.

"Da?" she called out. "Are you okay?"

"Go away, Siobhán." He sounded disturbingly non-belligerent.

"Uncle Seamus gave me some sports drink. Did you want some?"

"Just leave me alone."

This was bad news. The last time Da had missed a performance was when she was ten, when he'd had strep plus pneumonia, and then only because his doctor had drugged him nearly comatose.

She didn't know which she feared more—that he was too sick to take the stage, or that he felt well enough to try to play and made himself worse.

She waited a beat. "Da, it's okay if you can't play—"

"I'll be there. I-I just need to get past this." Sounds of wretching came from the room.

Shivawn swallowed hard. He was not well enough to go out. But how to get him to take care of himself?

Margaret came in behind her, and Shivawn glanced at her, knowing her worry sat stark on her face. Maggie shrugged with a helpless expression.

"Da, are you worried we'll fall apart without your beat? What about letting another drummer play with us? Zach from Taboo Soul—"

"I said *no*. We are the Kelly band, Siobhán!" Anger strengthened his voice. "We will take the stage as Kellys, or not at all..." A loud groan ended his diatribe, and his show of strength.

Stubborn idiot.

He was going to try to perform. Heavens, this was awful. The more she tried to talk him out of it, the more he argued he was going on. She shut her mouth, tagged Maggie in to try reasoning with him, and moved off to regroup.

A live feed of the event was on a television mounted near a corner of the ceiling. She sat down to think. Liam sat nearby, warming up on his muted mandolin. He seemed to be in his own little world, but from the occasional worried glances he sent between monitor and bathroom, she realized he was just as anxious as she.

The Beachies played. They seemed to be at full force, with electric bass, drum, guitar, and lead crooner. But when the wail of the high male vocal was supposed to come in, it was missing. She swallowed hard.

Not all the bands were affected—only those standing a chance of winning.

She wished she could be sure Townshend had done it on purpose. Then she'd have a focus for her fear and rage. Then Connor would have his justification. She wished even more fervently they could prove it. Then all the ailing musicians, her da included, would have justice.

She felt sick at the thought that Townshend might get away with this.

Rusty took center stage as soon as The Beachies were done. "The scale for tonight's contest is one through ten. Each judge will vote, then I'll ask the audience for their response, which will be measured on this." She whipped a hand toward a man-sized LED loudness meter mounted to the front corner of the stage. "All right. Professor Laufer, what did you think?"

"Good, but not as good as before. A seven."

"Ms. Lane, your vote?"

"They were sorely missing their falsetto vocal. Six."

Shivawn gave a snort. Marita Lane had an ear. Platt was utterly wrong with that crack about autotuning the other day.

Rusty began, "Mr. Platt—"

"What garbage! An original sound, but not anywhere near the purest surf music I've heard. Three."

Harsh. She crossed arms tightly, as if she could hold back her raging emotions that way.

"Audience?" Rusty threw her hand toward the throng on the dance floor.

They roared in response, clapping and hooting for a good five seconds. The meter's yellow lights lit immediately, quickly climbing into green.

Take that, Mr. Puckered-Asshole-Platt.

"The audience awards an eight, for a combined score of twenty-four."

More bands played. John, Jack, and Cherry left the green room, showing up on the monitor a while later. Rusty awarded more points. Shivawn chafed the whole time, gaze darting between monitor and closed bathroom door.

Finally Rusty announced, "Next, welcome The Harmonizers!" She extended her hand toward the second stage.

Shivawn's heart leaped into her throat and pounded double time. *We're next.*

"I'm going to go check on our set up," Cousin Margaret said. Liam nodded and followed.

On the monitor, a spotlight snapped on, cutting The Harmonizers' lead tenor out of the darkness. He took the mic and launched into the first words of "For Me and My Gal."

"That'll be our opening act." The bathroom door clicked open. Da stepped out.

Shivawn heaved a sigh of relief and stood.

Relief turned to horror when Da went sheet white, spun, and rushed back, slamming the bathroom door closed.

"Da?" she cried out. "Can I help you?"

The only answer was a groan.

She plucked out the sports drink, carefully opened the door, and set it inside. "This competition isn't that important. There will be others. We don't have to play."

"Don't be daft. Just give me a minute."

She paced, cursing the stubbornness of the Kellys.

"For Me and My Gal" finished. From the monitor, Rusty said, "That's a combined score of twenty-nine for The Harmonizers. Now, put your hands together for the Kelly Traditional Céilí Band!"

"Da. *Da.*" She spun back to the door. This was it. The actual moment where they had to get onstage or lose their place. She didn't want to disturb her poor sick da, but he'd never speak to her again if she didn't at least let him know. She slapped her palm against the wood. "They've *called* us."

A great groan and the door opened, revealing Da , green and sweaty. He plucked up the sports drink bottle from just inside the door, swaying a little as he cracked it and slugged back half the contents.

"Let's..." He burped. "Go." He shoved himself away from the door jamb, stumbling and nearly falling.

She grabbed his elbow, holding his sagging body. He'd always seemed so solid before, her rock. Yet now he felt light in her arms, and strangely frail. It scared her.

Then it galvanized her. No matter how invulnerable he thought himself, Paddy Kelly was only human. It was up to her to keep him from hurting himself more.

Yes, he was stubborn. She'd just have to out-stubborn him. *Out-Kelly him.*

"Da, it's simply not worth it. You're in no condition to go onstage."

"Y-you may be right." In a barely heard whisper, he added, "Mam, Da, I've failed ye." His eyes scrunched in pain.

Shock hit her, almost immediately dissolving in to distress. She'd never seen him like this. It shook her that the man who was always right, always running the show, was giving up.

She grieved for him. "You haven't failed them, Da."

"I wanted that recording contract for *them*, Siobhán. For your mother, and for you."

"For Kelly family history?"

"More." He clasped both her upper arms, panting. "This electronic-worshiping age, this tech-happy country. But our music is still valuable, still relevant—a big-name contract would prove it." A wave passed with gritted teeth. "I've seen how you feel about tradition, Siobhán." A moment, panting. "Shivawn." He nearly wept it. "I wanted the proof for my grandbabies."

Her heart bled for him. At that moment, she would have done anything to give her father what he yearned for.

"The Kelly Traditional Céilí Band," Rusty said again.

Shivawn's stomach dropped through her feet.

The spotlight came on and hit—an empty stage. Surrounding it, in the light-dusted shadows, were Maggie, Uncle Seamus, and Liam. More than half the family, all the melody and harmony they needed, but they'd lose their chance at making Da's dream come true. All because they were missing Da's bodhrán to drive them...

An idea that had been on the back burner began to boil again. Melody and harmony, and they just needed the drive?

Connor was perfect for that.

"Da." Shivawn seized her father by his shoulders. "You want that contract? There's a way to win it." *Win it all*, she realized, the future absolutely sparkling in her mind's eye. Connor would get his chance to play. Her da would get his contract. Maybe he'd even see how good Connor was, how happy he made her, and she could be with him without reminding Da of Annie.

"Final call," Rusty said. "The Kelly Traditional Céilí Band."

"W-we just need the d-drive, right?" Shivawn's excitement and need to get it all out before it was too late made her stutter out her idea of a fusion band. "So maybe Connor...or no, you're our drummer, so we need Zach to do drums...except then there's the reels. But see, I know Connor can do those..."

The way her words stumbled out, her ideas sounded half-stupid even to her. She should have picked up her fiddle and sung it.

Before she'd even come to a stuttering halt, Da's face had gone from white to red, not a real improvement on green.

"No! Weren't you listening, Siobhán? For the tradition to have meaning, *our* music must win. We take the stage as the Kelly band or not at all."

Her sparkling future shattered. Her heart wept, mirrored in the tears trickling down her cheeks. "B-but Da, if we combine, w-we can at least take t-tenth place. Otherwise, we'll have to f-forfeit—"

"Then we forfeit! But we do so as Kellys, not some Frankenstein's monster of a band."

Over the piped-in feed came, "Last call has passed. The Kelly Traditional Céilí Band forfeits and loses all claim on *any* of the prizes."

They'd lost everything.

Chapter Fourteen

Shivawn blinked up at Da, tears stinging her eyes and clogging her throat.

She had to face facts. She'd had a point, and a good point. Her father needed to rest, yet he wanted to win. Why not bring in a few substitutes? But the more poise she'd needed, the less she'd had as she stuttered and stumbled.

They'd lost, because she'd tried to explain her idea to Da and had blown it. And worse, he still wasn't getting the medical attention he needed.

Her clumsiness was getting in the way.

"Fine. Now that there's no reason to delay, I'm calling EMS for you and Aunt Katie." Snatching up her fiddle case, she stalked out of the green room. What the hell. He was going to yell at her no matter what she did. Might as well be for something she knew needed doing.

She'd just gotten off the phone with 911 when she met Connor mulling around the second stage. His drummer was setting up—with Maggie helping him, a besotted smile on her lips.

Shivawn blinked at them, her chest filling with tears for a different reason. At least Maggie had found happiness.

Connor's gentle hand gripped her shoulder, fingers strong and warm. She turned.

"Did something happen?" His gaze was sympathetic.

Haltingly, she told him about the fusion band idea. Shame and anger at her father's reaction mixed with passionate outbursts about how right her idea seemed to her, and her words stumbled out as much or more as with Da.

Meanwhile, behind them on the stage, The Battre was having the best set ever.

She finally stuttered to a halt, her passion spent. She slumped, oddly deflated and empty. "I didn't explain it well. You probably think it's a stupid idea."

"No." Connor's face lit from the inside. "That's brilliant."

"It is?" She blinked up at him. "Da didn't think so."

"One problem." Cousin Liam came up, toting his mandolin. "We finalled as the Kelly Traditional Céilí Band and Taboo Soul, not as the Taboo Céilí Band or the Céilí Soul Band or whatever the mishmash would be."

She set down her case and mulishly crossed her arms. "Doesn't change the fact that we finalled. *All* of us."

Liam shook his head and looked around. "Okay, so we have, what...? An electric bass, a fiddle, and a mandolin?"

"And a hammered dulcimer." Uncle Seamus strode up, face grim.

"And our light guy, Dan. I'm in," Connor said firmly.

"Us, too," Maggie called down from the stage.

"But it's your idea. Up to you." Connor searched her face. "What do you think, Shivawn? Do we do it?"

She gazed into his dark eyes. Steady. There for her. Heart hammering, she examined each of them in turn. She saw nothing but trust and hope. She'd stumbled and stuttered, but somehow, because she hadn't given up, she'd managed to convince them anyway? Wow.

But, now the big question. *Do we do it?* Can *we do it?*

If they didn't at least try, not only would the Kellys have lost, but Connor's band would lose, too.

And that bastard from The Battre would no doubt win.

Anger and a righteous fire ripped through her, screaming, *Yes!*

But Da had said no.

"I-I'm not sure." Her gaze fell to her shoes, blurring. "I don't know how to decide."

Connor stepped closer and bent to murmur in her ear, "What does your heart tell you?"

"Make the fusion band. But my head tells me to be loyal to Da."

Two fingers, slim and guitarist-strong, slipped under her chin and tilted her face up. Her gaze met his, dark and fathomless.

"That's not your head talking—that's your guilt. What does your head *really* say?"

"My head says..." Slowly the truth rose inside her, lifting her heart like a warm air current. "It says what it's been saying all along. Da's way is for *Da.* I have other music living, beating inside me."

"Yes." His eyes burned with an equal fervor. "And what does your *soul* say?"

She snatched up her fiddle case. "It says grab this chance. *Grab* it with both hands, don't let go, and *make music.*"

"Then let's make music." Connor grinned at her.

His smile was the sun, his faith in her warming and cheering her like sunrise.

"Right." She pointed to Liam and Seamus and Connor. "Onstage. Now, now, now! We're playing 'Cooley's Reel.' Connor, give the tempo to your drummer."

"You've got it." Eyes gleaming with pleasure and excitement, he leaped onstage while Uncle Seamus took his case behind the stage, threw it open, and took out his instrument.

Shivawn was about to join them—when Da reeled up.

His face was dripping, but his gaze burned with an anger she'd seldom seen, so deep and harsh it turned his eyes black.

"*Siobhán*. You'd betray the band by joining with our enemy? Betray our *family*?"

Chagrin banged through her, sharp as lightning. She knew he considered the band, the music, his love for family.

Making music wasn't about family for her. It was *about* the *music*.

She frowned. Having stuttered and stumbled before, trying to get him to see, she wasn't going to make the same mistake twice.

So she didn't try to change his mind but simply stood up to him with her own feelings.

"Da, I understand. I really do. But this isn't about family. It's not about me or you or even this competition. It's about the *music*. It's about living where I'm happy." She glanced at the stage, where Uncle Seamus was hooking up his dulcimer to an amp—smiling from ear to ear. This wasn't just about her happiness. This would liberate Uncle Seamus.

The Battre was banging out its final notes.

"Da, I've got to go."

"Siobhán Kelly. If you do this, you're not family any more!"

She turned to him, tears stinging her eyes. "Nor am I family any less, Da. Family just is. As is music. If you don't want to speak with me anymore, well, I guess I'll have to understand that. But don't ever think we're not family. When you and Mom separated, that didn't make you any less my da. Didn't stop me from being your daughter." She paused, then threw her arms around him. "You're my da, and I'll always, *always* be your daughter."

The EMTs arrived then, guided by Rusty, muscling through to Da. He tried to shake them off.

"Paddy Kelly." The club owner's tone brooked no nonsense. "Get on that gurney, you stubborn old fool. *Now*."

And miraculously, he meekly did as he was told. As Shivawn shook her head in amazement, he left with Rusty and the EMTs.

Shivawn leaped onto the stage to help Seamus. They set up in a fever of activity, fear and excitement colliding inside her, igniting new energy like a match. There was no time to rehearse, no time to check tuning or amp settings, no time even to alert Connor's light guy as to the change in songs.

There was only time to make music.

Shivawn stood on the darkened stage as she had a hundred times before, anticipation surging. But this wasn't the electric thrill of setting her heart on display or the joy of filling the hall or even the fear of making a fool of herself. Tonight Connor stood on this stage with her, helping her birth a brand-new creation.

What happened next might be wondrous, or they might crash and burn. But for this moment, five hearts soared with hers in anticipation of a sparkling future.

Chapter Fifteen

Connor had just helped Shivawn's uncle hook up his dulcimer to the amp and hadn't had time to adjust his gain and main much less the more specialized controls when Rusty's voice broke through.

"That was The Battre! Professor, what do you think?

"A sev—"

"A solid ten," Platt shouted. "That was the best sixties rock and roll I've heard *since* the sixties. Full points to The Battre, and I'd give them twenty if I could!"

The crowd shouted, a combination of cheers and boos. Connor took his place at Shivawn's side, drawing strength from her, sending her wordless support in return. She tipped a small smile at him, and it was the sun rising inside him.

"Thank you, Mr. Platt," Rusty drawled. "But it's not your vote yet. We'll get to you. Professor?"

Laufer stuttered, "Well, I...I guess it was good, for a sixties band. I'll give it a...a nine."

Connor's heart fell. Whatever score the professor had originally in mind, Platt's leaping in had skewed it.

"Ms. Lane?"

She gave it a nine as well. Platt jumped in with a shouted, "Twenty!"

The crowd roared again, so loud it was impossible to tell if it was support or denial. Rusty could barely keep order. Finally, she just shook her head. "The final score for The Battre is thirty-seven. Next is the last band of the evening—Taboo Soul!"

The spotlight hit Zach, but a little too low because they hadn't had time to check places. Connor's stomach went sour. Their nemesis had gotten a nearly perfect score.

And they didn't even have a full band. How could they pull this out of the toilet?

"Objection!" Platt shouted from the balcony before Zach could start.

Connor exchanged a quick glance with his friend, who twitched a stick toward the snare, a nonverbal, *"I can play over him."*

But he knew what Platt was going to say, and he wanted to get it over with, so he gave Zach a small shake of the head. His buddy shrugged but sat back.

Platt continued, "Who is *that* onstage? That band didn't go through the preliminaries."

Connor tipped his head in front of Shivawn's standing mic. "Actually, we did. *All* the musicians in this band were vctted in the earlier rounds."

Platt snorted, "That's no good—"

"Overruled, Mr. Platt," Rusty called. "He's right. All the musicians *are* finalists. And we want to hear music, not words. *Play.*"

Zach was smart enough that he took the cue immediately, hitting four rimshots to give the tempo. Then Shivawn came in with the tune. But Dan missed spotting her with his light.

Connor winced. Her music was brilliant, but half of the enjoyment for the audience was the fire of her performance. Taking the tune, seeing her dance with it, the gleam of merriment in her eyes.

But she played it in the dark, and his heart hurt for her.

Until he heard *how* she was playing.

Low. Mysterious. In her hands, the fiddle in the dark made that reel tune a sultry mystery. A promise of excitement to come, but unrevealed.

God. She's perfect. He loved her a little more in that moment.

And when he came in on the second phrase, he matched her with a single, teasing note. One tantalizing heartbeat to complement her mystery.

Was it working?

Platt, the judge who thought there was no good music after the Beatles, would surely vote them down. And Connor feared the others would be swayed. Including the audience.

And the audience...

Nobody moved on the dance floor.

Chapter Sixteen

No one's dancing.

Shivawn had known they were in trouble the moment the spotlight missed Zach—the poor light guy had probably been as surprised as Rusty when, instead of a five-piece band there'd been six mishmashed onstage. None of them had been in the spots he'd prepared for.

Then her place to start had come, and she'd been utterly in the dark and stayed that way. Worse, she'd known they were operating against a hostile judge ready to take the rest of their listeners with him.

Her stomach had taken a nosedive into her feet. *We're lost. There's no way to make this look planned.*

But with Connor standing near her, ready to support her...she'd realized there was one play. One chance to save them—but it was a long shot and everyone else would have to catch and follow her lead.

No pressure.

Still, she'd taken the chance. She'd started low. Inward. As mysteriously as possible. Hoping at least Connor caught it.

And then he came in with that low, softly snarling bass note. She knew how loud he could play, and this was nowhere near it. It was perfect. All potential power.

And she realized this wasn't a disaster, this was a dazzling *opportunity*. If they hadn't had this screw-up, she would have tried to recreate the joyful, one-dynamic blast of a céilí band. Connor might have tried to play it as psychedelic rock.

But they weren't a céilí band nor a rock-and-roll band. They were a fusion, which meant they had the potential of each, and more.

The whole could be greater than the sum of the parts.

So she played soft but began to tighten her vibrato, not a sad, sweet song, but the start of an emotional roller coaster only now ratcheting up the first hill.

Liam caught on first after Connor, adding a slow plucked arpeggio—which, because his instrument was mic'd, she could actually hear.

Uncle Seamus came in next, his hammered dulcimer added like ice cracking above the melody. Maggie joined them on the B theme, her flute plaintive, like the moan of the wind sweeping across a barren plain. And Shivawn thought, maybe, just maybe, they could do this.

But no one was dancing.

Why? Are they bored? Do they hate us? Scared, she sent her awareness out into the darkness. She could feel them out there, the audience.

Their stillness...was more of a hush. A silence, not from boredom or dislike, but from *expectancy*.

Excitement bubbled just below the surface.

Fear broke, and she began to dance, little steps. The light finally found her, just as Connor's bass began to drive them, faster and faster. Like a swirling wind, Maggie began cutting and sliding. Liam switched from plucking to strumming. Zach added impossibly fast flurries of drum strokes to the phrase joints.

Then Uncle Seamus's cracking ice broke—no, *blasted* apart. He started hammering the tune like a jackhammer.

The swirling wind became a tornado of sound. Faster and faster they went, louder and louder, until their music was a freaking force of nature.

And people *were* dancing out there now, dancing and shrieking and filling the floor with crackling energy and joy.

Shivawn played faster, better, more furiously than she'd ever played before. And faster yet, beyond the fastest she believed she could go, driven by Connor's force of will, voiced on his magnetic, charismatic bass.

Then Platt, as if he knew he had to do something now or, against impossible odds, they'd win—he shouted into the furor, "This is awful!" He screamed over their cascade of music. "Terrible!"

Her heart plummeted.

But the light guy, Dan, the one she'd thought was lost, proved himself. He provided a brilliant light show, yes. But one thing more.

He lit, not the stage, but the audience.

The entire space, not just the dance floor, was bubbling, shouting, cheering. As he ran his spotlights over the audience, the beams crisscrossed on joyous dancing, fists punching the air, and bodies popping like demented kangaroos.

Shivawn signaled the last time through. As she'd played it for Connor, as the Kelly band played it, the music came to an abrupt halt two beats from the end. Connor caught it and signaled the drummer.

Silence. She expected Platt's boos to fill it. If he booed, she didn't hear it.

Because the audience *screamed*. They loved it.

The band slid their final two notes into the screams. Shivawn felt awesome, vital and intensely alive, more than she'd ever felt in her life.

"That's a ten from the audience," Rusty shouted. "A *twenty!*"

"You brilliant *bastards*." Platt didn't even wait for the screams to die down or Rusty to cue him. "You fucking brilliant bastards."

The audience lapsed into stunned silence.

As the house lights rose, the critic's lemon face hit Shivawn like a wet towel. Her fiddle, which had been weightless just seconds before, felt awkward and heavy, and her bow drooped to her side. Sweat she hadn't felt in the heat of the moment chilled on her back and neck.

Brilliant bastards. Did that mean he liked them or hated them?

Connor, beside her, frowned, while Maggie half-turned with a questioning look at Zach. The joy drained from Uncle Seamus's face. Liam took a supportive step nearer him and scowled up at the critic.

"You fucking prodigies with your raw talent." Platt glared at them. Then he stood and glared at *her*.

She quailed.

"You have no idea how the rest of us feel. You don't know what it's like to work like a dog for every scrap of approval. To practice and practice and *practice* until your fingers are bloody, but you're never good enough."

All the sparkling delight drained from her, leaving her cold. She knew unfortunate musicians like the ones he was talking about, filled with music but unable to fully express it because they weren't technically adept. Good—but never quite good enough. Her heart hurt for them.

Connor frowned at her with a small shake of his head. Then, much like the night Platt had first eviscerated her, he rolled his eyes.

She felt her own widen in surprise. Then gratitude for his support warmed her, lightened her. With it came a realization.

I work hard. She practiced hours every day.

Yes, competition was fierce, and not everyone got the recognition they deserved.

But here, tonight, her practice had paid off, along with the countless hours the others had put in, to give the audience a unique, compelling performance they wouldn't soon forget. She stiffened her spine, not about to let Platt or anybody cheapen that fact.

"Five." Platt snarled it, sat with a thump, and glared at his compatriots. The audience rustled with whispers.

Five. No way they could win, now.

Her joy drained. She stood there, shaking. She'd expended a lot of energy worrying about her da and aunt, and now she'd spent all the rest playing. Nothing was left except trembling limbs and cold disappointment. She waited for Rusty to ask the other judges for their votes. Even if they'd enjoyed the music, they'd drop their scores to concur.

"Hell, no. That was a pure ten," Professor Laufer said. "Music? That transcended music to become an experience."

"Ten," Marita Lane agreed.

Shivawn blinked back tears at their support. Still, with Platt's five, they couldn't win. Rusty's twenty was a number shouted in the heat of the moment. The best they could do was thirty-five. That might beat the other bands, but it was still two short of The Battre's thirty-seven.

The spotlight moved to Rusty, crouched down to hear what Ben was saying. She stood. "Before I announce the winner, it has come to my attention that the Kramer Pharmacy had a theft Wednesday night. Stolen were a powerful emetic and a prescription-strength colon prep laxative. I noticed several of the bands were missing members tonight due to flu-like symptoms. Notably, these afflicted members all attended a party last night given by The Battre."

Shivawn managed a wan smile at Connor. Someone else had noticed Townshend's mischief. At least the little prick wouldn't entirely get away with it.

"So?" Townshend shouted. "Some people overindulged. Not everyone got sick."

Or maybe he would. She sagged again. Connor leaned nearer to her in support as Maggie went to stand beside Zach at his drumset.

"You deny that you poisoned those musicians?"

"I not only deny it, I can prove it. Our party was almost twenty-four hours ago. No laxative takes that long to work." Grinning, Townshend nodded around. As if he'd knocked Rusty's idea on its ass.

"Do you also deny you have a brother who studied pharmacology? That he could have made a time-release version of the drugs?"

Surprise tingled through Shivawn. She took her bow in the same hand as her fiddle and reached for Connor with her freed hand.

"M-my brother?"

Connor suddenly pointed into the audience. "Light *him!*"

The Taboo Soul spotlight swung to hit a small guy in a beard. The man flinched and started to run.

Shivawn grabbed Connor's hand and clutched it hard. Liam and Uncle Seamus moved a step closer to them.

The mountainous security guy in Starstruck black shoved through the crowd after Townshend's brother and grabbed him.

She exchanged a look with Connor. If the Battre had indulged in foul play, did that mean...?

"Who cares?" Platt shouted from the balcony. "Announce the winner of this farce. It's obviously The Bat—"

Rusty faced her own sound guy and made a throat-cutting motion. The judge's mic cut off abruptly.

"Mr. Platt is right," she said smoothly. "We need a winner. Audience, what do you think?"

Shivawn's heart beat harder as Rusty called out, "All in favor of the fusion band—?"

"You can't," Platt shouted naked-voiced from the balcony. "It's not fair."

Her breath disappeared, and she crushed Connor's fingers almost to dust.

"It's the only thing that's fair." Rusty turned on him with a glare that would've melted steel. "You gave an impassioned speech before, Mr. Platt, now let me give one. You sat up there and were disagreeable to your colleagues and badmouthed bands at every turn. Not only that, you were mean and rude and divisive. And your favorite band—don't think we all didn't notice who was your darling—was just as bad. This is my bar, my event, and I'm handing first place to two bands who didn't battle, but came together to give us the best music I've heard this whole week." She gestured at them.

Gaze sparkling with tears, Shivawn glanced around her. Maggie and Zach hugged, Liam pumped a fist, and Uncle Seamus thrust both mallets into the air. And Connor...

His black gaze came to her, warm. Proud. Fulfilled. She remembered his words. *"I just wanted to play at Starstruck one more time."*

Platt stood at the edge of the balcony and roared, "You revolting woman! The Battre won fair and square. Your miserable attempt to replace them with this misbegotten bastard of a band—"

"That's *enough*." Rusty gestured to security. "Please escort Mr. Platt out."

As they led the squalling judge down the spiral stairs, Rusty held up a hand. "That's it then. Pending further investigation, The Battre is disqualified. The winner of the Battle of the Bands is—Kelly's Taboo Soul!"

The audience's response to that was so loud, the LED meter lit immediately up to red. Rusty flicked off the mic and applauded, hands slapping in the high pitch of real appreciation.

Shivawn's heart soared. She clutched Connor's steady hand tight lest she float up to the sky. He raised their joined fists then held out his free hand for Maggie. She joined with him, bringing Zach with her. Liam jogged to take Zach's hand and Seamus wrapped his around Shivawn's fist holding fiddle and bow.

Her spirit singing, bathing in the approbation of the whole room, she bowed, the rest joining with her. Dan's joyous jouncing of spotlights celebrated it all.

Rising, tears of joy filled Shivawn's eyes, making the stage lights sparkle and shift in her vision. There was family, and there was music, and she'd be true to both.

But tonight, she'd found a new family, brothers and sisters in music, and had never been happier.

*　　*　　*

By the end of the summer, Kelly's Taboo Soul had completed its first album. Early buzz was stupendous. Shivawn was astonished when they'd landed an agent, courtesy of Rusty and demo tracks, who immediately started planning a global tour.

But school was due to start again. If not for Connor's steadfast presence, she might have gotten cold feet. Yet she remembered that, with his help and that of friends and family, she'd pulled off a miracle. So, holding onto his hand with a crushing grip, she phoned the head administrator to ask for a leave of absence.

She stumbled over her words and at first he said no, but, nearly crushing Connor's fingers, she kept at it. She turned the no into a maybe, which mention of the world tour turned into a yes.

The Clancys returned home to get ready for a long tour while Shivawn, Connor, and Zach got things together in the United States.

It wasn't more than a couple days though before Zach announced he was heading for Ireland for a quick vacation. "A Maggie vacation," Connor said to Shivawn.

Shivawn sighed wistfully. She hadn't seen her da since he'd left for the emergency clinic. She certainly hadn't spoken with him. She'd texted a few times, and Da snipped short texts back. She remembered how furious he'd been with her and worried.

So when Connor took part of his advance and flew them both to Ireland, she was surprised and gratified

But also scared.

Yet when she arrived, her father immediately hugged her like no time or harsh words had passed. Just as Uncle Seamus once said—Da was like a spring storm, all squalling fury but soon passing to sunshine and warm breeze. He made a bit of a fuss—and many disgusted noises—before admitting Connor could play with the céilí band. *"But he has to play a proper string bass!"*

Liam had a beat-up old double bass in his basement. Connor took it and made it sound like the Stradivarius of basses.

As they assembled together, Shivawn's heart soared just as high as at the Battle of the Bands all those weeks ago, but in a different way. There were families, and there was music, and in Kelly's Taboo Soul, she'd found a new family through music. But now...

"A *proper* string bass." Connor sighed as his left hand walked along the fingerboard of the upright bass while his right thumped the strings. "Kellys are the most stubborn creatures alive." His tone was long-suffering, but his gaze on her held a wealth of love.

Now, playing with her da, and her aunt and uncle and cousins, but also her lover and his friend—she found equal happiness in her musical family.

Da started the beat on bodhrán, joined by Zach on tambourine, the crossbeams of their musical foundation. Connor and Aunt Katie joined them the next bar, laying down the bass and chordal floor.

As she waited to enter, to complete the musical structure with the melody, her hand strayed to her flat stomach—and her gaze strayed to Connor.

He glanced at her with a quick warm smile.

Her whole being smiled back.

Before him, she couldn't see passing on any sort of family musical tradition.

Now she could.

Like her da, and his da before him, she'd someday teach her child family pride and honor along with the eighth notes. Because, though music was the subject, with Connor, the real lesson was love.

"Kellys, stubborn." Shivawn hit the downbeat, pretending to consider Connor's words as she danced her bow along the strings. "I don't disagree. But I'd have said resolute."

"Less talking," Da said. "More practicing."

She laughed. She opened her mouth to answer as she always did—and love and joy bubbled up inside her as the whole family answered along with her, a rousing unison, "*Yes, Da!*"

Continue reading for the first chapter from Hot Chips and Sand.

About Mary Hughes

Who am I? A lover of stories that crackle with action and emotion. A mother, a flutist, a binge-TV-watcher of NCIS, Elementary, The Flash, and Agents of SHIELD.

I write wickedly fun romantic adventure and scorching hot paranormal romance, fast-paced reads with challenging heroes—and resilient heroines who aren't afraid of a challenge.

Most of all, I'm a believer in grand passion.

I'd love to hear from you!

Newsletter
http://www.maryhughesbooks.com/Newsletter.html
Website http://www.maryhughesbooks.com/
Blog http://maryhughesbooks.blogspot.com/
Facebook http://www.facebook.com/MaryHughesAuthor
Twitter http://www.twitter.com/MaryHughesBooks

Hot Chips and Sand
© 2016 Mary Hughes

When American Skyler Jones is kidnapped, she manages a heart-pounding escape, only to be cornered in the hotel room of a lithe, enigmatic man. The kidnappers burst into the room, but the man hides Skyler by covering her body with his—and kissing her. Her kidnappers are thrown long enough for the man, known only as Cliff, to race Skyler through narrow streets and hide her on a boat going home.

Skyler thinks her troubles are over, but Cliff is really Sir Humphrey Hawkesclyffe, genius inventor of the next gen supercomputer. He's zeroed in on Skyler—he says for heading his software development team, business only. But as they work together, Skyler starts to fall for the lonely boy genius who's become a rugged man of action.

He seems to fall for her, too—at least their sizzling kisses suggest more than simple chemistry. But is Cliff just mixing pleasure with his business? And then the kidnappers come back for round two...but it's not Skyler they've come for this time.

Enjoy the following chapter from Hot Chips and Sand:

Skyler Jones was deep into coding a project her boss had shoved onto her last minute yesterday, due in two hours. She'd gotten her teeth into it and was thinking she might actually pull off a miracle and get it done, when said boss appeared in the opening of her cubicle like *Office Space*'s version of a grim reaper.

"Drop everything, Skyler. We have a new client." Phil Westerby smacked a letter on Skyler's desk. He cheerfully acknowledged his beer belly and three-hair comb-over was less a graceful slide toward middle age and more stealing the base. But his management style was all *Art of War.* "Rush-rush."

"They're all rush-rush." Skyler turned from her computer screen to give her boss her full attention. "You know I have at least three projects due this week, right? Including the one you gave me yesterday."

"Colonel Fahrrad takes priority." Phil thumped the letter in underscore. "Potential international client. Could be big money."

Irritation ruffled Skyler's nerves, the curse of a redhead's temper. Not that she bought into the stereotype, but she was a redhead, and she did have a temper. "Naturally, you'll forgive any of my missed deadlines."

"Would a little overtime hurt you? Besides, this is for a security system, the kind of project you love."

She stifled a sigh. Normally she did love her job at Fitzwater Software and Consulting. It was the perfect combination of meeting new people and problem solving. And she *wanted* to be helpful. "All right, let me take a look."

She lifted the paper. Good quality, with dented print like an impact printer or a real typewriter instead of a laptop and inkjet. Possibly the client had a secretary who simply loved the feel of an old-fashioned typebar, but more likely a client helplessly mired in the last century.

Reading the letter, she started getting a whole lot of bad vibes. "This Colonel Fahrrad already contracted with another vendor. Do you think the other vendor knows he's sniffing out the competition?"

"Sure. I think. Probably. Does it matter?"

"That he might be going behind the vendor's back?" A wave of annoyance made her clench her teeth. Like the high school guy who brought a girl to a dance, then left her alone so he could chat up other girls. Or fiancés who'd test-drive other models before he even got a woman off the showroom lot. Not that she had experience of that. Much. "Yes. I have to ask how serious this guy really is."

"Serious enough that I scheduled you to meet him today at two."

"The conference room is booked—"

"Boardroom."

That stopped her. Usually only upper management used the board room. "You must really want this client."

"The company president does. International, Skyler."

"That's nice." She pushed the letter back across the desk at him. "But I don't think I'm right for this."

"You know what I think? I think you have an appointment at two." He gave the letter one final thump and stalked away.

She closed her eyes for a moment to get her frustration under control. She prided herself on being professional, but sometimes, like now, it was hard.

Deep inhale. Breathe frustration out. Five of those and she felt calm enough to open her eyes. Time to do a little research on the colonel. She pulled up a browser and abruptly lost all the calm she'd fought for.

Boris Fahrrad had been secret police back when the KGB was cool. He'd been run out of several countries for archaic interrogation techniques.

In February of this year, he'd been hired by a progressive Middle East prince to help stabilize the small country of Middle Yemen.

Then, on the first day of June, Fahrrad staged a coup.

She sucked in a breath. That sure as heck explained the desire for a palace security system. He'd want to make sure no one would pull the same trick on him.

Checking dates, she saw that was only a week ago. This guy was a real winner, kicking out the old regime then off on a shopping spree within days.

Despite her churning gut, she put the two p.m. appointment in her calendar. Fitzwater had given her a job at her lowest point. Her loyalty couldn't be bought, but it could be won. If Jerry Fitzwater wanted this contract, she'd do everything she could to secure it, including meeting a scary dictator dude.

Besides, this was her job. While at one point, she'd dreamed of having it all, having a balanced life—a nice job, a nice family, even a nice house with a white picket fence— her fiancé had screwed that over when he screwed *her* over. Her career was all she had left.

She was very serious about her career.

Breathe in, push pain out. Turning from the deep pang of memory, she set her mind to finishing rush-rush project number two and clear the deck for the new number one.

A few moments later, her calendar chimed. She looked up, disoriented. She'd been deep in her work.

"Two p.m. boardroom" blinked on her screen.

"Two, already?" Panic goosed her to grab her phone and a client welcome folder then dash to the boardroom. She threw open the door to meet Colonel Fahrrad.

Seated at the long, glossy table was a slight man with a toothbrush mustache wearing an over-designed uniform and too-big hat. His beady eyes were glued to a sales brochure before him.

Her first impression was Classic Dictator ala *Mission Impossible.*

"Two-oh-one. You're late." He spoke without looking up. "Mr. Jones, the president told me you were the very best your company has to offer, but this tardiness does not speak well." His gaze rose. And stopped, shocked. "*Ms.* Jones."

As she introduced herself, he sat transfixed, gaze avid on her.

Because he was expecting a man, or did she have lunch salad in her teeth? She sat cautiously beside him.

"What an unusual color for hair." He reached out and grabbed a curl.

Alarm spiked her. She automatically swatted the strand from his grip.

His eyes sparked with thwarted anger. But he controlled himself, and actually smiled, with a toothy, gold-capped grin and a slight nod in apology.

Fighting to keep her professionalism, she began, "Your letter said you wanted a security system, Colonel Fahrrad. But you're already working with another company—"

"My predecessor's choice, sweeting. I wish to make my own alliances."

That actually made sense, but the endearment grated. She tried again. "Fitzwater doesn't do hardware, though. We specialize in database design and implementation."

"I am not worried about hardware, sweeting. Or anything hard." His slow, sensual grin sent frissons of unease up her spine.

If he hadn't been a potential client—scratch that, a potential *international* client, deeply desired by the president of the company—she'd have walked out. As it was, she asked politely, "What do you want the security system for? Your government headquarters?"

"For the entire country."

"Wh-what?" Surprise drove the word from her lips. "The technology for securing a bank or building exists, but a whole country...? Wouldn't your military be a better bet?"

"Middle Yemen is too small and too poor, sweeting. But *you* have exactly what I need." Again that oily grin.

Actual alarm goosed Skyler to her feet. She suppressed a shudder to slide him the welcome folder. "Tell you what. Have your people send us the specs, and we'll get you a quote. My card's in the pocket. Thank you for your time. I'll have someone show you out." She scrambled out of there and hoped never to see Fahrrad again.

Two days later, as she left work late, she was kidnapped.

Four men came out of the blue and plucked her right off the Boston sidewalk. Shock stunned her long enough for them to slide her toward the open back door of a black sedan. *If they get me in there, I may never return.* The dark maw disturbed her enough that she began to struggle. She wriggled loose and ran back toward the building but only got three steps before they caught her. Freaked, she did the first thing she thought of—she chucked her messenger bag into the nearest bush. She hoped someone would find it and know she was in trouble.

They stuffed her in the car. One held a out blindfold— and a gun. He didn't say a word, but the muzzle spoke for him quite clearly. She put the blindfold on.

Without sight, she got a skewed sense of time and place. Car ride. Being hustled through open space up a set of stairs. Sensation of intense speed and dropping stomach. Airplane? The drone of engine went on and on. With each passing moment her body got colder, and her mind floated farther away.

The riffle of cards. Her kidnappers broke their silence over what sounded like a card game. She didn't recognize any of the words, though.

Except one—Fahrrad.

That sent her stomach into shut-down mode.

Two stops. Three times she smelled food. Somewhere between twenty and thirty hours later, a door *shooshed* open, and she was pushed onto her wobbling legs into a wall of heat.

Her whole body went from ice to ash, no thawing in between. Trembling badly, she stumbled down clanging stairs onto tarmac so gooey it stuck to her shoes as she tried to walk. The air smelled of sand and spices and was so hot it hurt to breathe.

In the small, sane corner of her mind where she huddled, she remembered the saying "It's not the heat, it's the humidity."

Her lungs burning from the inside out, she thought, *No, it's definitely the heat.*

They removed her blindfold in a dank, sweltering room. Bed, small table, attached bath...it looked like a run-down hotel room.

One of the men shoved a dark blotch at her. But she only stared at it, hollow inside. Terror must've burned her out.

The goon shook the thing at her and spat some angry-sounding words. The blotch resolved as her eyes adjusted to a red teddy, mostly lace and air. Familiar.

Like the one she'd bought for her wedding night.

The guy shook the teddy again then pointed at her—with a gun.

In the hollow of her chest, anger sparked. She'd been harassed, kidnapped, threatened, and now was being rudely forced to wear an article of clothing she'd sworn never to put on for a man again.

The spark of emotion saved her from breaking down. She fanned her anger and felt a modicum of control return to her limbs. *Damn straight. I'm not gonna let a dictator with a bad hat and his goons get me down.*

Snatching the teddy, she stalked into the room's bathroom, a closet-with-toilet. As she changed, she searched the tiny room. The cabinet behind the mirror yielded a handful of bobby pins that she stuck into her hair—might come in handy for picking a lock, if she knew how to pick a lock. Still, doing something, anything, made her feel better, more in control.

She needed that feeling when she came out and they burned her own clothes.

"Hey, I might need those," she protested.

One had enough English to answer, "Not with the colonel." But they all leered in the international language of *yuck*.

She needed an escape plan.

First chance I get, I'm getting out of here.

As plans went, it was short on details. But her ears perked when one of the kidnappers patted his growling stomach. The wiry bilingual leader nodded, pointed at her, and barked a command at the smallest kidnapper, a thin youth barely past pimples. The youth scowled as the leader and the other two swaggered out.

Going out for dinner to celebrate, no doubt, leaving Scowly behind to guard her.

She gauged the kid's physique. Stringy but underfed. She probably outweighed him by ten pounds and had at least a couple inches on him.

She could take him. All she had to do was judge her moment.

Then Scowly cut considering eyes to her, licking his chops in a way that made her shudder. *Oh, no.* She crossed her arms over her breasts and mentally promised him dismemberment if he tried. *I'll fight. You may win, but not before I take thirty-five cents of your best hamburger.*

He growled but picked up a magazine.

Pressing a hand to her breastbone, she was surprised to feel her heart thudding hard and fast. That wouldn't help. She coached herself. *Deep breath in, press stress out.* Wait for the right moment.

She fisted hands and waited. And waited. She was ready to scream when her captor pointed to her and barked a word, probably "Stay," because he went into the bathroom and shut the door.

Yes. While he was relieving himself, she quietly let herself out.

She found herself in a narrow, airless corridor lined by doors. Definitely a hotel or boarding house. To her right, the corridor ended in a wall. To her left, it ended in a door.

Picking the door direction, heart pounding, she ran.

The door opened to a narrow, airless stairwell, hot as a chimney. Wood stairs. If anything had told her she wasn't in the USA anymore, Toto, those rickety wooden stairs were it. She crept down, panting heat like sandpaper, trying not to get splinters in her bare feet.

A switchback flight emptied into a well with *two* doors. The one before her probably led to another dank corridor. Swallowing dry, hot air, she chose the one behind.

It opened onto a lobby. Her heart soared. A lobby meant an exit, people, maybe even a police force. She took a couple steps into the room. Wall cubbies were stuffed with mail. A couple rickety chairs sat on cracked linoleum.

The door shut behind her, revealing a large curled-up orange triangle in the corner. Modern sculpture? She stopped for a moment, trying to calm her frightened panting, and stared at the bizarre art sitting mid-dirt.

The outside door banged open. The three kidnappers returned just then, bearing bags wafting spicy odors. Carryout.

Heart nearly exploding from her chest, she scoured the room for a place to hide, but the rickety furniture wouldn't conceal a praying mantis, much less her.

She spun and took to the stairs.

Adrenaline rocketed her up a half-flight before the searing heat leached all the strength from her. Legs stuttering, she forced herself to trot up the second half-flight to the original floor, ears straining for shouts of discovery and a slammed door below.

Nothing.

Passing the landing, a stitch grabbed her ribs as she started up the next half flight, slowing her to a limping walk.

This was not good. Her mind screamed at her to run, but her body screamed at her to slow down, rest. The hours of sitting, the terror, the killing heat, had eaten away most of her strength, and that panicked run had drained what was left.

Palm on the wall, she stopped mid-flight to bend over, panting. "I am strong," she told herself firmly. "I work out. I am reasonably healthy. And above all, I am *not* panicking..."

A shout from downstairs made her heart skip.

She started leaping steps two at a time. Cracked plaster walls flew by. She tried to remember her pep talk.

Not panicking. So what if kidnappers are chasing me? It's no worse than Phil hounding me for his TPS reports. An absurd image of her boss, his spindly arms toting a gun Rambo-style as he demanded his reports, distracted her from the growing stitch in her side. But the pain grew until she thought she had a burst appendix.

Pausing on the third floor landing, she held her cramped side, puffing breath. "I am strong," she coached herself. "I work out. *But not in hundred-degree heat.* "Definitely reconsidering...the all...Cheez Curlz diet."

Bam-bam.

Skyler froze, all her muscles clenched as she strained to identify the sound.

Thudding, rhythmic. Feet, hitting the stairs below. Damn it, her opportunity to escape, blown sky-high. Well, what did she expect, with her elaborate plan consisting of R, U, and N?

Hiding place. Panic goosed her to leap up stairs to the fourth floor landing.

Where the stairs ran out.

"Fry my motherboard." She scanned the small space. A ladder hung from the wall, and a hatch perforated the ceiling. Grabbing the ladder, she nearly beaned herself pulling it down. Lug the ladder into position, climb it with her trembling limbs, all before the kidnappers caught her?

Not happening.

She spun and ran back down the stairs. She'd made the second floor landing—just as the door flew open.

Throwing herself behind it with raised hands, she suffered a whack to her shielding forearms. As the door swung closed, she saw the legs of two kidnappers running up the stairs. Heads indicated two were running down.

Arms smarting, stomach churning, she followed the legs as the lesser of two evils. They turned past the third floor, continuing up. She followed cautiously. Peeked around the switch just in time to see one pair of feet disappear through the fourth-floor door—while the other stood guard.

Searching top to bottom while the other pair searched bottom to top? And they'd meet like a pair of clapping hands in the middle, trapping her.

Still, what choice did she have? She tiptoed back to the third floor landing. Panting, she cracked the door.

A dungeon corridor stretched before her, even danker than the second floor. It appeared carpeted in a sluggish river of blood and walled with a corpse's teeth.

She blinked. Her eyes adjusted to the low watt bulbs, and the hallway resolved to a dirty floor with a ratty red runner and chewed plaster walls picketed by narrow wooden doors. None of the teeth—er, doors—shouted, "Hide here."

Fighting to control her thudding heart and trembling limbs, she slid through the door into the hallway. Her mind clicked through and discarded possibilities as fast as a multicore processor. Open closed doors, possibly meet more goons.

Run back downstairs, *definitely* meet the kidnappers.

If only this were a computer game. A save game would be nice about now. Or a pause button. Why didn't life have a pause? Then she could try each of those doors, restoring each time one opened to a monster.

But no. If she screwed up, it'd be *Game Over.* Her stomach knotted.

Shouting. Footsteps on the stairs pounded down. She glanced back at the stairwell door, her throat tightening.

Hide. Didn't matter what might be behind the room doors, she definitely knew what was flying toward her in the stairwell. With a deep breath for courage, she scurried to the first door on the left and cranked the yellowed glass knob.

Locked.

"Smack me with a Dell." Rattling the knob did no good, nor did kicking the door, which, since her feet were bare, stung her toes. She hopped around, trying to bring the pain under control, remembered *Game Over,* and hobbled across the narrow hallway to grab a second door knob. She turned and pushed.

It gave.

She half-ran, half-fell into the room, slamming the door closed behind her, her chest heaving with relief.

Hiding place. Skyler scanned the room—and froze.

Standing mid-room was a giant.

Half-naked. Sun-bronzed chest. Very, very male.

And staring at her with eyes so blue they were pure cobalt fire.